A Hole in the Fence

Christian Fiction for Kids

Diane Lil Adams

This is a work of fiction.
All the characters and events
are the result of the author's imagination.
Any resemblance to actual persons,
living or dead,
is purely coincidental.

*

All the glory to God
and all my thanks to Tank

This book is dedicated to my
GrandGirl Extraordinaire
Phoebe Christine Clark
who wielded her red pen
with diligence and wisdom

*

For he does not willingly bring
affliction or grief
to the children of men.

- Lamentations 3:33

Prologue

The elderly woman came out onto the balcony
and rested her arms on the warm wooden railing.
She was slightly tall for her age, with silver hair
and pink glasses which she wore on a chain. Her
name was Margaret Cameron, but her grandgirls
called her Meemaw. She baked the best chocolate
chip cookies in the Universe, because she was
allowed to borrow recipes from the Divine
Cookbook.

Three stories below, her husband was busy
removing twigs and leaves from a tiny culvert that
diverted the rain away from the miniature roads

that zigzagged across the garden. His earthly name was Walter Cameron, but nearly everyone called him Pops. He was nearly as tall as his wife, but he had a lot less hair and his was white.

They both had remarkable blue eyes that twinkled like Christmas lights when they were pleased. They were both very easy to please.

Pops looked up when Meemaw appeared, almost as if she had sent a secret signal. He raised a hand in greeting, then tipped his head, asking her a familiar question.

Meemaw laughed and nodded. *Yes*, she told him silently. *I baked a batch of chocolate chip cookies and set aside a whole jar just for you.*

Pops was caretaker of the "old Templeton place." His job didn't pay well, by human standards, but it included a few special privileges - Pops could eat as many cookies as he wanted without ever getting sick or fat. Since it was Meemaw's job to care for the caretaker, she baked at least one batch of chocolate chip cookies every day.

Meemaw turned her head so she could observe the drama about to take place next door. A boy of eleven had come out to sit on the back step. He was a tall boy, but just now, he was hunched over, as if a heavy weight had settled on his shoulders. He bowed his head, his sandy-colored hair hiding the tears that were threatening to spill from his pretty green eyes.

Meemaw hated to see children suffer. She was glad she would get to help Neal find his hole in the fence. She began to listen with increased concentration, so she would know exactly what she was meant to do.

"Neal!" someone called from the front yard, but the boy only shook his head.

"Neal!" came the woman's voice again, more insistent this time.

He raised his hands and covered his ears. His mother's voice was strained with grief, but Meemaw knew it sounded like anger to Neal.

The woman strode purposefully over the grass and began to lecture the boy, because he hadn't answered when she called. Though her words were blurred by distance, Meemaw knew what she was *really* asking. She wanted Neal to say he understood why she was going away without him. She had forgotten that a child cannot understand an adult's reasons, just as an adult cannot understand the reasoning of God.

Chapter One

Neal stood and faced his mother, his fingers curled into fists of frustration. Angry words were exchanged until the young woman held out her arms for a final hug.

"I just wanted to tell you good-bye," she said sadly.

Neal turned and fled across the neatly mown lawn, into the club house his dad had built when he was a boy. He sat down on a large rock and removed his glasses, carefully wiping the lenses with the hem of his T-shirt. He would not cry! He would be strong and brave, like his father had been *before* he was killed at the World Trade Center on 9/11.

A car started and Neal froze. His mother was leaving for California, to stay with her parents until she could begin to heal. Neal was a miniature version of his father. She couldn't take him along without being reminded of the tragedy every time she glanced in his direction. Neal would remain in

Missouri, with his father's parents. His mother hoped he could comfort his grandparents as she could not.

Neal wondered why no one seemed to think *he* needed to be comforted. Was it supposed to be easier to lose your father than your husband or your son? What if his mother never came back? What if he was stuck here forever, with two people he barely knew? They were so formal and polite all the time! How had his dad turned out so friendly and so much fun after growing up with such serious parents? There were pictures of his father scattered all around the house, but Neal never heard his grandparents mention him. Were they pretending he was still alive?

They hadn't come to New York after 9/11. They never saw the ruins of the skyscrapers that made it impossible to pretend.

Neal replaced his glasses and stood up, gazing out the door of the clubhouse. On the other side of a cornfield, he could see the tall house that belonged to the neighbors his grandmother described as "strange." Their clothing was out of style, their car was old and spotted with dents, their house looked like it might collapse any minute. They were friendly to everyone, almost like small children who don't know any better.

Mr. Cameron spent most of his time working in a garden that was hidden behind a tall privacy fence. Mrs. Cameron spent most of her time on the third floor balcony, watching him. No one understood how they could afford to buy the old Templeton place. Some suspected they had won a lottery. *They seem the type to gamble*, Neal's grandmother had sniffed with disapproval.

Their granddaughter lived with them, though no one knew why. Rose was an odd child, given to outlandish behavior, and Neal was advised to avoid her. On the other side of his grandparents' house was a subdivision where plenty of "normal" children lived. *Go and make friends with them*, his grandfather had suggested.

Neal wasn't sure whether his behavior had ever been described as "outlandish," but he knew it wasn't "normal" either. He was curious about the Camerons - was it possible that they were criminals? Maybe the girl wasn't really their granddaughter. Maybe they had kidnapped Rose and were holding her for ransom. Maybe that's how they got the money to buy the old Templeton place - kidnapping children for a ransom. While he was here, he would keep an eye on these strange neighbors, watching for questionable activity. If he saw the girl with ropes tied around her wrists or a chain fastened to her ankle, he would think of a way to rescue her. Maybe if he could become a hero, like his dad, his mom would come back for him.

Neal stretched out on the floor of the clubhouse with his hands pillowed behind his head. He imagined himself far into the future, after he was grown up. He wouldn't go to college or have a career and he wouldn't get married or have kids. Maybe he wouldn't even have any friends. He would travel, never remaining in one place for more than a few weeks. People would ask his mom where he was and she would have to say, "I don't know! He keeps disappearing!" He would wander around the world, doing odd jobs for people, making just enough money to buy food and a new pair of shoes now and then. He wouldn't even tell anyone his real name. After a while, he would probably *forget* his real name.

He heard a whirring noise, and lifted his head to look out the door. There was something suspended there, something so white, it was nearly iridescent. It was bobbing up and down as if it were on a string. Neal sat up to get a better look, and it immediately disappeared.

"What was that?" he asked aloud, fascinated in spite of himself.

It was probably some kind of small bird that only lived in the Midwest. Maybe he should go inside and ask his grandfather if he'd ever seen a bird like that. Maybe he would find his mother sitting at the kitchen table, chatting with his grandmother. "Oh, Neal!" she would say. "I turned around and came back. You didn't unpack yet, did you? I want you to go with me after all."

Neal got up and dusted off the back of his jeans. If he promised to be careful, maybe his grandfather would allow him to borrow the binoculars that hung on a hook in the study. He could keep an eye out for the bird, and keep an eye on the Camerons at the same time.

He found his grandfather in the living room. He stood before him and described the bird in a scientific manner, then waited politely for his grandfather to comment.

The elderly man scratched his head with a perplexed expression. "A bird might stray out of its normal range, or be blown off course. Given its size, it could be a hummingbird. Pure white? Maybe an albino hummingbird? I don't know, Neal. I'm no ornithologist."

Neal's grandmother had come to the door to listen. "There are some nature books upstairs," she told him.

"They were your father's," his grandfather explained, staring hard at the newspaper he had folded across the arm of the chair. "There might be a bird book among them."

"Be sure your hands are clean, so you don't dirty the pages," his grandmother cautioned.

"And be careful with the binoculars," his grandfather added.

Neal went to the kitchen and washed his hands, then went upstairs into his dad's old bedroom. Without looking around too much at anything else, he chose four books from the bookcase. Fetching the binoculars, he returned to the clubhouse. He sat cross-legged on the floor with one of the books spread opened across his knees. He turned the pages slowly, studying the pictures, making a note of any bird that was very small or colored with large areas of white. Maybe it wasn't a small bird, he decided after a while. Maybe it was a large insect.

He trained the binoculars against his eyes, slowly turning his head as he scanned the treetops. All he saw were grey squirrels and brown sparrows. Finally he ventured out of the clubhouse and wandered around the yard, moving slowly and quietly.

Just when he was ready to give up and go inside, there it was again! He stood perfectly still, wishing he could catch it. It was bigger than a bug, but smaller than a bird, and incredibly white.

His grandmother called that dinner was ready, and the tiny creature flew off.

Neal wondered what it would be like to be the sort of boy who didn't go in when he was called. He could disappear into the woods behind the clubhouse and hike off into the wilderness. His grandparents would get frantic when it grew dark and he still hadn't come back. They would call his mother on her cell phone and she would wonder if something bad had happened to him. She would feel guilty for leaving him behind and immediately return to join the search. When he finally allowed himself to be found, she would tell him how sorry she was that she hadn't taken him with her to California.

Neal went to the clubhouse and gathered the books. He wondered whether his father had ever seen a little white bird, or bug, and if he had persuaded his parents to buy the books so that he could try to identify it. The thought brought him some comfort.

Chapter Two

Rose sat by herself in the very last seat on the school bus, studying her reflection in the window. If she turned her face to the left, she looked like ten-year-old Rose. If she turned it to the right, she looked like her grandma, the same grandma who had given her a home permanent the night before.

After squirting the stinky solution on the left side of Rose's head, Meemaw had been interrupted by a phone call. When she returned, she absentmindedly doused the left side again. As a result, half of Rose's dark hair hung as straight as a ruler, while the other half was as short and matted as sheep's wool. Naturally, this unusual hairdo had earned her a lot of unwanted attention at school.

Rose folded her hands and closed her eyes. Her lips started moving, but no sound came out of her mouth. "You say we don't get what we want because we don't ask, so I'm asking," she pleaded silently. "I need a friend."

Rose wasn't chatting with an imaginary person,

as her classmates suspected. She was praying.

"I don't care who. It could be that girl who wears her brother's old T-shirts, or the one who brings salsa and chips for lunch. I'm not asking to be popular. I just want one person I can talk to. Meemaw is great, but please, could You find someone closer to my age?"

She paused for a moment, to decide if there was anything else she needed to mention. There was no point asking God to fix her hair, since everyone had already seen it. And she had already prayed for her mother, as soon as she woke up, before she even ate breakfast.

"Okay, that's all for now," she finished cheerily. "Thanks for listening."

Some children would be afraid to talk to God the way Rose did, but Rose had been taught to believe that God loved her, and that there was nothing she could ever do to cause God to *stop* loving her. She always spoke to Him with respect, because He was, after all, the Creator of the entire universe. But she wasn't afraid to ask for things, or to let Him know when she was feeling sad or impatient, or just plain mad.

When she opened her eyes, she realized that a number of her fellow students had turned backwards in their seats to stare at her.

Nothing so irritates our enemies as showing them kindness, Meemaw had reminded her this morning.

Rose forced a big smile, hoping it counted as kindness.

Nicole Macavity pointed at her and started

laughing, and soon, all the other kids were laughing too. Nicole was the most popular girl in the whole school. She had blond hair and blue eyes and all the right clothes. Everyone, except Rose, wanted to be her best friend.

Nicole had started making fun of Rose the minute she began attending David City Public School. The first day, Rose had merely walked into the classroom, stowed her book bag under the desk, and sat down. She hadn't tripped or run into anything and she hadn't spoken one word to anyone.

"Why did they have to put her in *our* class?" Nicole had muttered, loud enough to be heard by everyone except the teacher. "Don't we have enough losers already?"

Rose had been surprised by Nicole's words - how could someone hate you before they had even met you? Rose pretended she hadn't heard. She was pleasant to Nicole, and to everyone else. She smiled all the time, she offered to help people with assignments and she even gave away a few of Meemaw's chocolate chip cookies.

But it was all for nothing. Every day, Nicole said mean things about Rose and all the other kids laughed. Rose knew they were scared *not* to laugh. If they didn't do what Nicole wanted them to do, she might start making fun of them too.

One day, after weeks of tolerating Nicole's cruelty, Rose finally decided to fight back. Two weeks ago, she had marched up to Nicole in the cafeteria and asked why she was being so mean to someone who had never done one single, solitary unkind thing to her. Nicole sputtered and her face turned red while she tried to think of an answer.

Then Rose did something unforgivable - she giggled. She always giggled when she was nervous, but she couldn't explain that to Nicole Macavity. It was definitely the worst thing she could've done. She watched Nicole's eyes turn squinty and realized she had only made things worse.

The bus arrived at Rose's stop and she stood up and walked quickly down the aisle to the front. She pretended she didn't hear the other kids laughing and snorting.

"Hey, Rose," Nicole said in a syrupy voice. "We were just wondering - Are you a half-wit? Get it? *Half*-wit?"

Before Rose could even try to think of a clever answer, a large white insect dove through the bus window and burrowed into Nicole's blond curls.

Nicole shrieked and raised both hands to her head, thrashing her perfectly permed hair into a nest of tangles. Her book bag toppled to the floor as she jumped from her seat and began dancing in the aisle, screeching for help. "Get it out! Get it out!" she cried hysterically.

"Quiet down!" the bus driver yelled. He shifted the bus into Park, and turned around to see who was causing the ruckus. "What's your problem?" he demanded, rising and heading in Nicole's direction.

"There's a bug in my hair! A huge bug!" Nicole cried, her eyes wild with terror.

Rose felt a twinge of guilt for not offering to

help. *Love your enemies and they might become your friends,* Meemaw often said. But Rose didn't want to be friends with Nicole Macavity. She did wish Nicole would invite her to go bowling or ice skating someday, but not because she wanted to actually go. "No thanks," she would say. "I'd rather change a baby's poopy diapers."

Rose watched as the bus driver studied Nicole's head, latching his hands behind his back.

"Get it out! Get it out!" Nicole shrieked.

"I don't see anything," the bus driver told her.

"Get it out or I'll tell my father!" Nicole warned him in an icy voice.

Fortunately, the bug chose that moment to emerge from Nicole's hair and sail off through the window again.

"Probably a ladybug," the bus driver said with disgust. "All that hoopla over a little ladybug."

As Rose hopped down the bus steps and skipped across the street, she could hear some of the other students laughing. And for once, she was pretty sure they weren't laughing at her.

Chapter Three

Rose walked slowly down the long driveway that wound through the giant tulip trees in front of the old Templeton place. Nearly every tree had at least one branch that Rose could reach, and she loved to climb them, nearly to the top, and watch the clouds drift by. The grandparents had given her permission, so long as she didn't hurt herself, or the trees.

Though Rose missed her mother and prayed every day that she would get well, she didn't really mind living with Meemaw and Pops. They didn't own the old Templeton place - they were just caretakers, but that didn't matter to Rose. She had lived in small apartments and tiny trailers the first ten years of her life, so she felt blessed every time she "came home" to the Templeton mansion. It was four stories tall, counting the basement, with hallways going every which way, leading to rooms and closets and more hallways. The Templetons had once been the wealthiest family in the county, but had lost their fortune and moved away, leaving the estate to fall into ruin. The roof needed new shingles, the shutters were loose, the sidewalks were cracked and there were squishy soft spots on the front porch steps.

"Ta dum!" a young voice chortled. Rose's cousin, Alexandria, suddenly leaped from behind a row of bushes, her arms spread nearly as wide as the grin on her face. "Lucky you!" she announced. "I've come to spend the long weekend."

"How come? I mean, no one told me," Rose said, noticing the way Alex was trying not to look at her hair. Alexandria was her favorite cousin, since they were almost the same age and Alex was generally good natured. They looked very much alike, with dark hair and solemn brown eyes and muscular bodies that rarely got tired.

"No one knew," Alex explained. "My parents were suddenly called away."

"Who called them?"

Alex lifted her shoulders. "My dad's business, I guess. We actually have school tomorrow and I'm going to miss an important test, but my mom wrote a note that I was needed by someone in the family. That's the way it is when you go to a private school - they're more understanding about situations like this."

Rose didn't like being described as a "situation." She suspected Meemaw had called Alexandria's mother and the two had declared Rose's failed perm a family emergency. All the same, she was glad for Alex's company.

The two girls trudged along side-by-side until

Rose stopped and shrugged off her back pack, allowing it to dangle from one hand. "Go ahead and say it," she dared her cousin.

"Your hair looks awful," Alex said obediently. "What happened?"

Rose made a face. "Meemaw went to church to do the newsletter and the secretary told her how Nicole Macavity got her hair permed and it turned out sooo cute that all the other girls decided to get their hair permed too. So Meemaw decided I ought to have a perm, but when she found out how much they cost ..."

"Like, seventy dollars," Alex said, fluffing her own permed curls.

"Yeah. So she bought a home perm to surprise me."

Alex scrutinized Rose with a serious expression. "Maybe your hair just doesn't take a perm well. I've heard of that."

Rose shook her head. "When Meemaw was half done squirting on the stinky gunk, she got a phone call. Then, when she came back, she forgot which side she did and accidentally did the same side twice. If she had asked, I could have told her, but how was I supposed to know she was only supposed to do each side once? Then the double dose started burning my head and I had to rinse it out quick. She was worried my hair was gonna fall out."

"Lucky *that* didn't happen," Alex said.

Rose nodded in agreement. "The truly sad part of the story is - I didn't want a perm! Now Nicole Macavity thinks I was trying to copy her. As if anyone with intelligence would want to be anything like Nicole Macavity."

Alex made a circular motion with her hand and Rose turned around, giving her the view from all angles.

"You need to get a tight perm on the right side of your head, so they match," Alex suggested.

"It still costs seventy dollars, even if you just want a half of a perm. Meemaw called and checked."

"Worse things could happen," Alex said, sounding very much like an adult.

"And they probably *will*," Rose sighed. "Though they can't get much worse than my mom being in the hospital practically forever. Not to mention that I've never even met my own dad."

"Steven was *like* your dad," Alex said cautiously.

"True, but he broke off their engagement and ran away," Rose reminded her. "I probably *scared* him away. Meemaw says I should have more faith, but ... How come everything goes so good for you all the time? You don't have more faith than I do and even if you did, it's easier for you to think everything will turn out good because it always *does* turn out good for you."

"Not always," Alex objected. "Remember that time when my tooth got chipped?"

"So what? It was a baby tooth. It fell out a couple of months later."

Alex lifted her hands and raised her shoulders. "I can't help it if I'm lucky. It's not my fault."

"My mom used to say we make our own luck,"

Rose remembered. "So that sort of makes it sound like it *is* your fault which means it's *my* fault that everything goes wrong for me."

"Meemaw should've let you stay home from school until you could get it fixed," Alex changed the subject.

"I figured it was better to go and get it over with," Rose said glumly. "You think it would help if I washed it a hundred times?"

"I doubt it. It would probably just make it frizzy. Did everyone make fun of you?"

"What do you think?" Rose forced a little laugh, as though it didn't matter.

"You should've told them what happened, so they could sympathize. You only make things worse with your attitude." Alex crossed her arms and shook her head. "I have a lot of friends, Rose. *A lot* of friends. And it's not just because my parents are rich," she added sternly. "Kids don't like to hang out with someone who is crabby. You have to be upbeat and happy if you want to be popular."

"Not everyone *wants* to be popular," Rose said.

Alex sniffed. "People only say that if they're not."

"No, it's true," Rose insisted. "I think it would be a nuisance to have a lot of people calling me every night to discuss whatever happened that day. 'Oh, did you see what "Susie Straight A's" was wearing?'" she mimicked the tone of someone judging her classmates with a critical air. "'Did you hear what "Bobby Blue Ribbon" said when Teacher asked him to add two plus two?'"

17

"We don't do that," Alex said crossly.

Rose tossed her backpack over her other shoulder and resumed a slow walk towards the house. "Here's what I don't understand: Nicole Macavity is the most popular girl in the fifth grade. Everybody wants to be her friend."

"Everybody except you," Alex reminded her.

"So why does she make fun of *me*? It's not like I'm the competition. How come the popular people go around making fun of the unpopular people? I mean, they're already popular, so what good does it do them?"

Alex didn't answer. She crossed her arms and kicked a rock, then she sighed and looked at Rose. "So, what do you want to do this weekend?"

Rose climbed the stairs to the porch and settled on the wooden swing that hung from the ceiling on rusted chains. She pushed with her foot until the swing swayed gently from side to side, creaking noisily. "I think I want to try out my paint set."

"You mean you haven't tried it yet?" Alex said with surprise. "I figured you would've used up all the paper by now. My mom and I went to about thirty stores trying to find it that big."

"Sixteen by twenty-four," Rose said with satisfaction. "Thanks. It's perfect." She knew Alex and her mom had also been the ones to find the paint set that included thirty-two colors and a packet of assorted brushes. The birthday tag said it was from Meemaw, but their grandma wasn't much of a shopper.

"Pops spent hours making you that easel," Alex

told her with a touch of disapproval. "I'll bet his feelings are hurt that you haven't tried it."

"A painting is only as good as its subject," Rose said absently. "And since I'm not allowed to go into the garden, what am I supposed to paint?"

The garden was a large tract behind the house, landscaped with trees and bushes and flowers, cobblestone paths and park benches, bird houses and bird baths, fountains and miniature waterfalls. Pops, their grandfather, spent practically every minute of every day tending the garden, with occasional help from Meemaw. Though Pops and Meemaw spoiled all of their grandchildren in every other way, none of them were allowed to put one foot inside the garden. Naturally, they were obsessed with curiosity about the area that was hidden behind the tall privacy fence.

"I asked my parents why we're not allowed to go in the garden," Alex said. "They say it's because they don't want us to trample the exotic flowers."

"If all of the grandkids were here visiting and we wanted to *play* in the garden, that would make sense," Rose said. "But not when there's just the two of us." *Or one of us*, she added silently. "So long as Pops went with us, he could keep saying, 'Be careful where you put your feet! Watch out for that exotic plant!'"

"True," Alex agreed.

No use debating the issue any further, Rose lectured herself. Meemaw and Pops would not bend one inch when it came to allowing the grandgirls into the garden.

"So maybe I'll paint a picture of you," Rose teased her cousin. "Meanwhile, we'd better go in or they'll think I missed the bus."

"Anyway, Meemaw's worried that you might've had a really bad day, on account of your hair," Alex remembered.

"No worse than usual," Rose said, trying to sound lighthearted.

Chapter Four

"I'm worried something will happen to you and since I don't know my way around in the garden, I won't be able to find you on time to save you," Rose said. Her fear wasn't entirely make-believe. If something happened to the grandparents, what would happen to her?

"I'm worried too," Alex tried to help.

"This girl at school? Her little brother fell off the roof and nobody found him for two hours!"

"He fell off the swing set, not the roof," Meemaw corrected Rose, without looking up from her knitting.

"You know him?" Rose said with surprise.

"I don't actually *know* him, but someone told me about his accident. He's going to be fine, by the way."

"Yes, but what if that happened to you?" Rose persisted.

Meemaw laughed merrily. "I never go on the roof!"

Rose clenched her teeth for a moment. "I'm thinking about if you go work in the garden when Pops isn't home. You could trip over something and fall. A person can trip over just about anything. A tree root, or a big clump of grass."

"I even tripped over a shadow one time," Alex said. "I thought it was something on the floor so I tried to step over it but it must have been *my* shadow because when I moved, it moved too."

Rose glanced at Alex and they both frowned. It didn't seem that their latest plan to get into the garden was going to work.

"How sweet you are to worry over me! Both of you!" Meemaw said, smiling first at Alex, then at Rose. "But I don't ever go into the garden when Pops isn't home. And he doesn't ever go into the garden when I'm not home," she added, before they could say another word.

Rose gave up. She popped a final bite of soggy chocolate chip cookie into her mouth and drank her milk, keeping the glass tipped until the dregs of the cookie crumbs slid down her throat. "Yum. Thanks, Meemaw."

"Yeah. Thanks, Meemaw," Alex agreed, reaching for just one more. "You make the best chocolate chip cookies in the whole world."

Meemaw laughed. "I don't know about that, but I'm glad you enjoyed them. Now put the jar in the pantry, under that checkered tablecloth, where Pops won't find it."

"We don't mind sharing," Alex said, sounding very mature.

"He has his own jar," Meemaw explained.

"*Had*, I should say. He polished them all off a little while ago."

Alex and Rose stared at the jar of cookies - it was a huge plastic jar, packed very full.

"Was it the same size jar?" Alex wondered.

"Yes it was, so don't feel sorry for him."

"If I ate that many cookies, I'd puke," Alex told Rose a few minutes later, as they climbed the stairs to the second floor.

"Pops never gets sick," Rose said, dropping her book bag just inside the door to her bedroom, where it would remain until Monday morning. Rose always did her homework during free time at school, since she didn't have any friends to talk to. "He eats about a hundred cookies every day. Sometimes he eats three pieces of chocolate cake. *Big* pieces."

"I hope I inherited Meemaw's baking talents," Alex said, stretching out on top of Rose's bed. "Where are we gonna sleep tonight?"

There were five guest rooms on the second floor, and the girls were allowed to sleep in any of them, so long as they cleaned up their mess the next day.

"Maybe upstairs," Rose said thoughtfully. "On the balcony."

"They wouldn't let us do that," Alex scoffed.

"Probably not, but maybe." Rose knew her grandparents felt bad about her hairdo so it was a good time to ask for special privileges. She exchanged her skirt and blouse for a pair of jeans and a T-shirt that said "Keen Kid," then stood before the mirror to study her reflection. "What did Meemaw say to you about my hair?" She had seen Meemaw take Alex aside and whisper in her ear.

Alex sat up. "I'm supposed to convince you to let Pops go buy another home perm so she can curl the right side."

"I'm scared something worse will happen," Rose admitted.

"Like what?" Alex said.

Which told Rose just how bad Alex thought it was. "Let's go up on the balcony and watch Pops for a while, want to?" she suggested.

"I'll tell Meemaw," Alex offered, jumping up and heading down the stairs.

Whenever the grand-girls wanted to sit on the balcony, their grandmother came along to "keep them company." Rose thought it was part of the garden mystery, but Alex thought it was just typical grandmotherly behavior - Meemaw was probably afraid they would lean too far over the railing and fall off the balcony. The truth was, sometimes the grand-girls grabbed Meemaw's elbows because they were afraid *she* was going to fall off.

Rose went to the door that hid the stairway to the third story and twisted the knob, surprised to find it unlocked. Though she knew she should wait, she stepped quietly into the stairwell. For some reason, it made her think of the night her mother went away.

Rose had already fallen asleep, but she woke up when she heard her mother yelling at Pops. Pops was so mild-mannered and gentle, Rose hadn't thought he could ever make anyone angry enough to yell. He said something back to Rose's mom, but Rose couldn't quite make it out. Then her mother shouted, "They aren't real! They aren't real!"

Rose wanted to know what her mother meant. *What wasn't real?* She was afraid to ask Pops. She didn't want him to know she had heard the argument and she didn't want him to worry that she was going to have a nervous breakdown too.

"Where's Rose?" Meemaw said outside the door.

Rose sat down on the first step and tried to look bored.

"Oh, there you are," Meemaw said happily. "Alex said you want to go on the balcony?"

"Do you mind?" Rose asked politely.

"Not at all. I just put the potatoes on so we have about half an hour before I mix the biscuits."

Rose went first, holding the banister as the stairs became steeper and more narrow. She didn't understand why Pops didn't rebuild them, to make them safer. He said he didn't understand why they hadn't been built safer to begin with.

At the top of the stairs was a long, skinny room with sloped ceilings and wooden floors. Like the attic of any old house, it was full of upholstered chairs sprouting tufts of stuffing, antique trunks filled with musty-smelling quilts, boxes of broken toys, old lamps with frayed black cords, and a variety of odds and ends that most people would throw into the trash.

Meemaw went straight to the French doors,

which were always propped open, and stepped onto the balcony. She leaned on the railing and squinted in the sunlight, gazing around in search of Pops.

"Be careful, Meemaw," Alex cautioned.

"Thank you," Meemaw said, stepping back a few inches, tucking her hands into the pockets of her sensible denim skirt. "I don't see Pops. I wonder where he's gone."

Both girls joined her at the railing, searching the garden for their grandfather. There were so many bushes and trees that could hide the stooped figure of an elderly man, especially from the third floor.

"I don't see Pops, but I see someone," Rose said, pointing her finger beyond the fence, beyond the cornfield, into the yard of the neighbor next door.

"It's a boy!" Alex said, leaning over the railing for a closer look. "He's going into the Simmons's shed!"

"That's because he's their grandson," Meemaw explained. "His name is Neal and it isn't a shed. It's a clubhouse."

"I didn't know they had a grandson," Rose said with surprise. "I didn't think they had kids."

"They had one son," Meemaw explained. "He was killed last month, on September 11, when the airplanes crashed into the World Trade Center."

"Really?" Alex and Rose said in unison.

"Really," Meemaw said sadly. "His mother is having a hard time getting over it, so she brought Neal here to live with his grandparents for a while."

"How'd you find out about it?" Rose asked suspiciously. She knew that Mr. and Mrs. Simmons didn't talk to Meemaw or Pops, even when they practically ran into them at the grocery store.

"I heard it from someone who knows them very well," Meemaw answered vaguely. "Pops and I are worried about Neal. He lost his father in such a tragic way and now it must feel as if he's losing his mother too. Do you think you girls could try to make friends with him this weekend?"

Rose inhaled noisily. Maybe she hadn't lost either of her parents in some dramatic tragedy, but that didn't mean she wasn't suffering. She wondered why nobody ever urged their children to be nice to poor Rose, whose mother was in the hospital. "Will he be attending David City Public School?" she asked.

"Most likely," Meemaw said.

"What's he like?"

"He reads a lot." Meemaw smiled, probably because she knew that Rose also loved to read.

Rose considered this. What if they liked the same books? Maybe he'd want to share a seat on the bus and get together after school to do homework and study for tests. Maybe they could meet on the playground during recess, talking about the tragedies of their young lives. Maybe Neal was the answer to the prayer she had prayed on the bus.

"Do we have time to go and meet him before dinner?" Alex asked.

"I think it would be best to wait until

tomorrow," Meemaw said, but she was obviously pleased by their willingness.

"I guess when he watched the Twin Towers collapse on TV, he kept looking for his dad," Rose speculated.

"I don't think I'd mention that," Meemaw advised.

Rose sighed. She knew it wouldn't really matter what she said or didn't say. He wasn't likely to want to be friends with her once he realized what a "loser" she was.

"We'll go over tomorrow, first thing," Alex said brightly. "Maybe we could invite him on a picnic."

"I'll have plenty of turkey for sandwiches," Meemaw promised. "And I told Pops I'd bake another batch of chocolate chip cookies in the morning."

"Meemaw," Rose said thoughtfully. "Isn't all that sugar bad for Pops? I mean, don't old people catch some kind of disease from eating too much sugar?"

"Is that right?" Meemaw said with a touch of concern. "Could you look it up on the intercom and tell him about it?"

"You mean the 'Internet'?" Alex asked, pressing both hands over her mouth to smother a giggle.

Chapter Five

Neal sat on the floor of the clubhouse, surrounded by books about insects and birds. His father must have been very interested in the subject, judging by the number of nature books Neal had found in his room. Since their New York apartment was on the 17th floor, the closest Neal ever came to nature was squashing a bug in the bathroom.

He had been studying the pictures all morning, but found none that resembled the bird or bug he had seen the day before. He wondered if it could be a whole new species, or possibly one already considered extinct.

Neal stacked the books neatly in a corner and sat perfectly still, listening to the absence of noise. In New York, it was never this quiet, not even in the middle of the night. In order to drown out the noises from the street below, his mom always turned on the TV, even when she wasn't watching it.

His dad had liked to listen to music, thumping his palms on his thighs as he kept time with the beat. Neal smiled, as he remembered how his dad would grab his mom and waltz her around the room, making her laugh.

He wondered if Mr. Cameron had ever seen the little white bird, but he didn't think his grandparents would like it if he went next door to chat with their strange neighbor.

A few years ago, Neal had stayed with his grandparents while his parents attended a seminar. Though no one had mentioned the topic in his presence, he knew it was meant for couples who weren't getting along. He was just as tired of the arguing as they were, but he would rather they keep fighting than get a divorce. He almost made himself sick with worry while they were away, which made his grandparents nervous and cross.

His grandparents were the kind of people who wore clothes that needed to be ironed, even when they weren't going out. They had expected Neal to be neat, clean and quiet. Several times a day, they had urged him to *go outside and get some fresh air, but please do not get dirty*. He had mostly stood around in the yard, watching for his parents to return, though they weren't supposed to come back until the end of the week.

The third day, the neighbor from the old Templeton place came around the corn field, pulling a wagon filled with neatly sawn boards. Before Neal could run inside to ask his grandparents what to do, Mr. Cameron asked him to help unload the lumber.

"What's it for?" Neal asked, biting his lip.

"Your dad's clubhouse," Mr. Cameron had explained, indicating a sort of shed in the back corner of the yard. "A few of the boards need replacing. I brought you a hammer and nails too. Just hang on to 'em when you get done. Maybe they'll come in handy some other time."

While Neal watched, the older man leaned the boards against the back fence, then handed him the hammer and a box of nails.

Neal remembered his dad talking about the hours he had spent in the clubhouse with his friends, but he hadn't realized it still existed. "Thanks," he told Mr. Cameron. He was pretty sure his dad would be pleased if he fixed up the clubhouse, though he wasn't sure how his grandparents would feel about it.

The day his parents were due to return, Neal's dad suddenly appeared in the doorway of the clubhouse. He looked around with a happy grin, and complimented Neal on an excellent repair job. The minute Neal stood up, his dad grasped him in a wonderful hug that said everything was going to be better from now on.

And it *was* better, even if his parents acted like they were making a movie, always whispering and laughing about stuff that didn't seem funny to him. When his father got killed, Neal couldn't help wondering about the order of events - why should his dad get killed just when he and Neal's mother were falling in love again? She wouldn't be nearly as sad if they had still been fighting all the time. It would've made it a lot easier on everybody.

Neal stood up and stared out the clubhouse door, wishing the rare bird would appear again. He should've taken his mother's advice and brought his Game Boy and iPod along. He was old enough to know that time moved faster when your mind stayed busy. His grandparents didn't even have a computer! How was he going to keep his mind busy when there was nothing to do and no one to talk to? Keeping busy was a lot more important since his dad died. And now that his mom had left him behind ...

At first, Neal and his mother were certain that his father had survived. He might be buried beneath the rubble, but the rescue workers would soon dig him out. He would probably have some injuries, but nothing that wouldn't heal.

Three weeks went by before his mother finally said the words out loud - *your father isn't going to be rescued*. Neal refused to believe it, even though he had been to the site and seen the tons of rubble still to be removed. He told his mother that he was going to go on thinking that his dad was alive. She lifted her hand, then let it fall, as if she were too tired to argue.

After that, Neal and his mother didn't talk about his father anymore. Neal went back to school and his mother went back to work. They avoided the routes that would take them near the disaster site. They didn't watch the news on TV, threw the newspaper away without reading it, and changed the subject if anyone mentioned Ground Zero in their presence. When they met at the dinner table, they talked about TV programs, or the weather, or

32

the dog who lived in the hallway.

One night, Neal told his mother that the dog had ridden the elevator with him that morning. When they reached the ground floor, it went to the front door and waited for someone to open it. The doorman told Neal that the dog would come back and sit patiently until someone let it in again. Then it would trot across the lobby and stand on its hind legs and push the elevator button. Neal thought this was a particularly interesting aspect of the dog story, but his mother acted as if she hadn't even heard him.

"I'm going to California, to visit my parents," she said.

"Am I going along?" Neal asked nervously.

"Not this time," she apologized. "You're going to stay with your father's parents."

"For how long?" he asked, trying to act as if it wasn't a big deal.

"I don't know," she said. Then she got up and began clearing the table.

They left the next morning and arrived in Missouri two nights later. Neal knew he would be staying more than a week this time. He was afraid he might be stuck here forever.

Suddenly the bird appeared, hovering over him for a few seconds, then soaring to the uppermost branch of a maple tree. He stepped back, slowly, trying not to blink. It was a bird, he decided, but *what kind* of bird? If only it would come a little closer, so he could get a better look. Instead, it fluttered away and landed in a small dogwood tree. Neal moved slowly in its direction, watching from the corner of his eye. He wished for a net, or at least for a video camera. When he stopped and tilted his head, to get a good look, the bird lifted off and glided to a large leafless branch on an otherwise healthy tulip tree.

It almost seemed to be luring him towards the house next door, though he knew that was a silly thought. He followed again, to prove his own theory wrong, but it kept moving nearer and nearer to the old Templeton place. "Maybe it's an escaped canary," Neal thought, edging further into the Camerons' yard. He wondered what Mr. Cameron would say if he caught him prowling around on his property. Would he remember Neal and the time he had given him the materials to fix the clubhouse? Would he offer him a net, or better yet, offer to help him capture the little white bird?

Chapter Six

"You'll have to do it," Rose told Alex. "If I knock on their door, they'll call the police." She gestured at her hairdo.

"The interplanetary police," Alex suggested with a giggle.

"Ha ha," Rose said without smiling. "I wish we hadn't promised Meemaw we'd make friends with this boy." She led the way around the cornfield, so they could knock on the back door, as Meemaw had recommended. "I feel stupid asking some boy if he wants to go on a picnic with two girls he hasn't even met. Betcha his grandparents won't let him, even if he wants to. His grandparents hate our grandparents."

"Why?" Alex wondered. "How could anybody not like Pops and Meemaw?"

"They *are* kind of strange," Rose admitted reluctantly.

"I don't think they're strange."

"You're just used to them. If you weren't used

to them, don't you think you'd think they were strange?"

Alex mulled it over, kicking clods of dirt with the side of her shoe. "Different," she decided. "They're just different from ordinary grandparents. Hey, look!" She darted behind the corn stalks. "Over there! By the fence!"

Rose peered in the direction she was pointing. The boy, Neal, was standing on the foot brace of a shovel, boosting himself at least eight inches taller. His face was pressed against the fence, as if he had discovered a hole which allowed him to view the forbidden garden.

"Wonder if he can see anything," Rose said hopefully.

"Rose!" Alex chastised. "We can't let him spy on the grandparents!"

Rose had inspected every inch of the fence line, searching for a knothole or crack that would allow her a glimpse of the garden. She only hoped he had discovered something she had missed.

"Let's sneak up on him," she said, hoping they would get close enough to see the hole in the fence before he heard them approaching. She stepped into the cornfield, and brushed away a cob web, moving between the rows with Alex close on her heels.

They were hot and itchy by the time they reached the other side. "Why didn't we just go around?" Alex groused with irritation, swatting at the gnats that were buzzing around her face.

"Shh!" Rose cautioned, sticking her head out and peering down the fence line. "I guess he heard us coming and got scared off," she said with disappointment.

"I guess he heard you coming, all right," said a young male voice. "The *whole neighborhood* heard you coming."

Both girls looked up - Neal had lodged the shovel between two large rocks and stood balanced on the handle, right in front of them.

"Scared off," he snorted, crossing his arms like Peter Pan. "I'm gonna be scared of two stupid girls?"

"*We're* stupid?" Rose retorted, feeling stupid. She shook her head, to try to get rid of the gnats. "You're the one who's about to get arrested!"

"Arrested?" he laughed. "For what? What law did I break?"

"You were looking through a privacy fence," Alex pointed out. "That makes you a peeping Tom, and that's against the law."

He shook his head with disbelief. "You're even stupider than I thought!"

"We *were* going to invite this snotty boy on a picnic and try to make him feel welcome here," Rose said, lifting her chin.

"We *were* going to share our grandma's chocolate chip cookies with him," Alex played along. "She makes the best cookies in the entire universe, but *he'll* never get to taste them."

"Like I'd eat anything your grandma made," he laughed. "It's probably poisoned."

Rose could tolerate people making fun of her, but she didn't allow anyone to make fun of Meemaw. Without warning, she grasped Neal's ankle and tugged hard.

In a show of loyalty, Alex reached for his other ankle, but only managed to catch hold of his sock.

"Hey!" he yelled, flailing his arms. "Leggo!"

Before any of the three could change their minds, Neal fell, pulling them all to the ground.

"I think you broke my leg," he said, scowling at Rose while he rocked from side to side, his fingers wrapped around his calf.

"Serves you right," Rose said, but she was worried.

"He's faking it," Alex told her. "He's scared he's gonna get in trouble, so he's faking it."

"I AM NOT SCARED!" Neal yelled, with a rage that seemed out of proportion to the accusation.

Before either of the girls could recover enough to yell back, something appeared in front of Rose's face. It was small and white and had wings. It hovered briefly, darted into Neal's face, then Alex's, then disappeared, all within the blink of an eye.

"What kind of bird was that?" Rose cried. She had instinctively crossed her arms over her head.

"It wasn't a bird," Alex said, looking around for it. "It was too small to be a bird."

"It was a hummingbird," Rose informed her.

"It was white," Neal said. "There's no such thing as a white hummingbird."

"It could be an albino hummingbird," Rose argued.

"It wasn't a bird, it was a butterfly," Alex said.

"Butterflies don't hover," Neal objected. He

turned loose of his leg and stared into the treetops. "It was a moth. A lunar moth."

"A lunar moth?" Rose repeated.

"Lunar, as in moon," Neal explained, rising to his feet and brushing the dirt off his shorts.

"I know what lunar means," Rose growled, standing up too, noting that she had a nasty scrape on her elbow.

"It was so strange," Alex said, still seated on the ground. "The way it buzzed each of us in the face."

"I know," Rose agreed. "Like it wanted to get a good look at us."

"There's a whole bunch of them," Neal said. "In there." He gestured at the fence with his thumb.

"Really?" Rose said with sudden interest. "You could see them?"

"I found a hole in the fence," Neal explained. "I've been watching them all morning."

Rose looked at Alex and Alex looked at Rose.

"What else did you see?" Alex asked.

"Nothing that needed a fence to keep it private," Neal said defensively. "Trees, bushes, flowers, bird houses."

"Bird houses," Rose repeated. They knew about the little houses Pops liked to make. They were occasionally allowed to paint them with bright shades of blue and purple and orange and pink.

"A whole bunch of bird houses," Neal said, taking off his glasses, polishing the lenses with the hem of his T-shirt. "I can't believe you attacked me like that," he added, sounding as if his feelings were hurt.

"I can't believe you said something bad about my grandma," Rose said indignantly.

"I can't believe you found a way to see through the fence," Alex said. "Think you can set the shovel back up, so I can have a look?"

"Why don't you just go inside the fence and explore?" Neal asked. "That's what I'd do."

"We're not allowed," Rose said, even while she tried to wedge the shovel into place.

"You're not allowed to go in your own back yard?"

"It's not really ours," Alex explained. "It belongs to our grandparents."

"It's not even really *theirs*," Rose said reluctantly. "They're just caretakers." Satisfied that the shovel was stable, she climbed onto it, stretching until she could press her eye to the hole. "All I see is bushes," she complained.

"We probably scared them away," Alex said with a shake of her head.

"Yelling like that," Rose agreed, glaring at Neal over her shoulder.

"You yelled first," he reminded her. "What happened to your hair?"

"Nothing," she snapped, jumping down. "I'm trying to start a new fad."

"At my school, everyone dyes their hair with Kool-Aid," Neal said, making a face.

"At your *old* school," Rose corrected him.

He stared at her with confusion.

"Aren't you going to go to David City Public School now?" she asked, wondering if no one had bothered to tell him.

"Maybe," Neal shrugged. He backed away from the fence and gazed up at the Templeton mansion. "So, do you really live here?"

"*I* do," Rose said with a touch of pride. "Alex is just visiting."

"Alexandria," Alex introduced herself properly. "And this is my cousin, Rose. Your name is Neal, right?"

He nodded. "How do you know so much about me?"

"Our grandma told us. She said ..." Rose stopped herself, observing Alex's expression. "She said you were going to be visiting your grandparents for a while."

"How would *sh*e know? I'm sure my grandparents didn't tell her."

"Because they're such big snobs," Rose said, ignoring Alex.

"I know," Neal said. "But you've got to admit, your grandparents do act sort of strange."

Rose and Alex eyed one another with serious expressions, then they both began to laugh.

Alex stepped up on the shovel and took a turn to peek into the garden. "One thing I think is so weird," she commented, the words slightly garbled as she pressed her cheek against the fence. "How come so many bird houses are on the ground?"

"He probably just didn't get them put up yet," Rose said. "Poor Pops. He's always saying he can't keep up with everything."

"I don't think he's planning to put them up," Neal said, resting his chin on his fist. "They're arranged like a little town, with roads going all around the garden ... at least the part that I could see."

"Yeah!" Alex said, sounding excited. "There's sidewalks and little fences. You can't see any of this stuff from the balcony."

"I want to see!" Rose pleaded, moving up behind Alex, so Neal wouldn't think he got the next turn. She hadn't seen anything like that when she looked through the hole, but she had mostly been looking upwards, hoping to catch sight of the white bird.

"Yikes!" Alex cried softly, jumping down and picking up the shovel. "Here comes Pops! If he finds out there's a hole in the fence ..."

The three children ran to the edge of the cornfield and Neal drove the blade of the shovel into the earth while Rose and Alex looked on with interest. The garden gate opened behind them and Pops came out, pushing a wheelbarrow filled with weeds and grass clumps.

"Howdy Doody, you three," he called cheerfully. "How about that corn? Gonna be as high as an elephant's eye one of these days."

"What should I say if he asks me what I'm doing?" Neal whispered.

"Digging worms," Alex suggested.

"Don't lie," Rose warned them both. "Pops can always tell if anyone's lying."

"Where's the closest place to go fishing?" Alex asked, when their grandfather stopped beside them.

Pops made a funny face while he thought it over. "Depends on whether you're gonna fish for trout or bass. Did you know that trout can ... or is it salmon? Anyhow, one of them swims upstream, which isn't easy." He laughed, and the three children laughed with him. "'Course, you could just go fishing in the creek."

"What creek?" Rose and Alex asked together.

He gave them a puzzled frown. "Haven't you ever been down to the creek?" He pointed to the steep slope behind the garden. "Only takes about five minutes going down. Takes a good twenty coming back up. Does me, anyway."

"Are we allowed to go there by ourselves?" Alex asked.

"Don't know why not. Water's not very deep, even after a good rain."

"What about snakes?" Rose said. She was petrified of snakes. "I bet there's a million snakes around a creek."

"There are no snakes," Pops said with such total certainty, Rose believed him. "And if there's anything else that scares you, I'm sure Neal will frighten it off. Won't you son?"

Neal looked surprised. "Well, yeah," he said.

"We could take a picnic lunch," Alex suggested with enthusiasm.

"My grandma's got turkey for sandwiches," Rose remembered. "Unless you're worried it might be poisoned."

Neal gave her a sheepish grin.

"Their grandma makes the best chocolate chip cookies you ever tasted," Pops told Neal. "You wouldn't want to pass up the opportunity to try them."

"I guess it's better if I don't go home first," Neal

thought aloud. "But if they call me to come in and I'm all the way down at the creek ..."

"I'll tell them where you are, if they call," Pops promised. "But I'm pretty sure they won't call till about the time you get back."

"I'll go ask Meemaw to pack us a lunch," Alex said, turning and running towards the front yard.

"Want me to put the shovel over by your clubhouse?" Pops offered, giving Neal an understanding smile. "You won't be needing any worms. 'Bout the only thing you could catch down there is crawdads. Rose, you want crawdads for supper tonight?"

"Yuk," Rose said predictably. She knew it was Pops's way of saying, *No more spying!*

Neal placed the shovel across the debris in the wheelbarrow. "Thank you," he said.

"You're welcome," Pops said happily. "Have fun at the 'crick'!"

"Isn't he nice?" Rose said softly, staring after her grandfather with a look of devotion.

"He is pretty nice," Neal agreed. "But how come he won't let you go in the backyard?"

"We don't know why," Rose said. "When we ask, they just smile."

"Don't you think that's kind of strange?"

"For sure," Rose agreed. "But you know, strange isn't always a bad thing. I mean, don't you ever get tired of the way everybody dresses exactly alike and has the same favorite color and likes the same stupid movie?" It was her way of finding out whether Neal was one of the popular kids at his school.

"Everybody's scared," he explained.

"Scared of what?"

Neal shrugged. "That people will laugh at them."

"Well, I'm not," Rose said boldly, fluffing her hairdo with both hands.

Neal didn't say anything for a minute. "Maybe you make friends easily so it doesn't matter if you look strange," he told her. "But not everybody is that lucky."

"No, I guess not," Rose sighed. If he knew the truth about how many friends she *didn't* have, he probably would cancel the picnic. Or just go with Alex and leave her behind.

Chapter Seven

"How was the picnic?" Meemaw asked. She was sitting in a rocking chair on the balcony, her knitting project temporarily forgotten in her lap.

"Good," Alex told her. "Neal says a lot of people eat crawdads."

"Yes, they do," Meemaw agreed, smiling at Neal. "Were there any snakes, Rose?"

"We didn't see any," Rose admitted. "But there was a beehive."

"It was a hornets' nest," Alex corrected her.

"It fell," Rose said with a shiver.

"But Neal grabbed a stick and rolled it into the creek," Alex said, beaming at Neal.

"Bees can't swim, can they?" Meemaw asked.

"They didn't drown," Rose explained, aware that Meemaw didn't like it when they killed things. "They just came out of the nest and flew away, all together in one big cloud. The sandwiches were yummy," she added. "Thank you for fixing them." She leaned on the railing and let her eyes search the garden for the tiny white bird.

"Yeah, thanks," Alex said, looking pointedly at Neal.

"That was the best sandwich I ever tasted," he said obediently.

"And that's a real compliment, coming from a New Yorker," Meemaw said with satisfaction.

"Meemaw," Alex said, joining Rose at the railing. "Have you ever seen something in the garden that looked like a giant white butterfly, but flew like a hummingbird?"

Meemaw sneezed, and drew a handkerchief from the pocket of her apron, pressing it over her face for a moment. "Fireflies?" she suggested.

"Fireflies?" Alex and Rose said in unison.

"You know, lightning bugs," Meemaw explained. She blew her nose and tucked the handkerchief away.

"It was too big to be a lightning bug," Rose corrected her gently. "And anyway, this was during the day."

"I think it was a lunar moth," Neal said with some authority.

"A lunar moth?" Meemaw said, looking up at him. "What an interesting theory."

"Their body is white and their wings are pale green, which could look white in bright sunlight. And I think they can get as big as a hummingbird."

"Wouldn't they be nocturnal too?" Alex asked him.

"I think so, usually. But there are always exceptions to the rule."

"Yes, indeed there are," Meemaw said. "To every rule, don't you think?"

Neal nodded, with a very serious expression.

"So," Meemaw said, finding her place and beginning to knit. "Did you see it today? The firefly?"

"It wasn't a ..." Rose shrugged and gave up.

"Meemaw?" Alex said, meeting Rose's eyes. "Do you think Rose and I could sleep out here on the balcony some night?"

"I don't know why not," Meemaw said. "There are some sleeping bags in that cabinet by the door."

Alex and Rose only stared at one another, too shocked to speak.

"You *will* promise not to do anything dangerous and get hurt?" Meemaw said without looking up.

"Sure! I mean, of course not," Alex said quickly.

"Of course not," Rose agreed. She looked over at Neal and saw the look of disappointment on his face. "Umm, Meemaw? I wonder if you'd care if Neal slept over?"

"I wouldn't, but I don't imagine his grandparents would allow it," Meemaw said with sympathy.

Both girls turned to look at Neal. They could tell by his expression that Meemaw was right.

"I'd better go," Neal said, checking his watch. "I haven't been back since morning."

"They've been looking for you," Meemaw told him. "They even went out to your clubhouse."

"Why didn't you say so?" Neal sputtered. He didn't seem to realize how rude he sounded.

"Just now," Meemaw explained gently. She indicated the clubhouse with a point of her knitting needles and all three children gazed beyond the fence. Mr. and Mrs. Simmons were just emerging from the shed-like building, looking left and right in search of their grandson.

Neal started away, then hesitated. He went to Mrs. Cameron's rocking chair and stooped down so that his head was on the same level as hers. Then he turned to look across the balcony.

It was impossible to see his clubhouse without standing up.

"You have such a scientific mind," Meemaw commented.

Neal opened his mouth and closed it again, as if he couldn't think of anything to say.

"Won't you get a backache if you sleep on the floor?" Alex worried, watching Pops roll out his sleeping bag. "My mom always says she gets a backache if she doesn't sleep in a decent bed."

"Not me," Pops said with good nature. "I can sleep anywhere."

"Sometimes he falls asleep at the kitchen table," Rose told Alex. She let her head roll back and her mouth hang open while she shut her eyes and made a snorting noise to demonstrate.

Pops laughed along with Alex and climbed into

his sleeping bag. "I'm going to trust you girls not to get into mischief," he said, fidgeting until he felt comfortable. "'Cause if you do, I'm the one who'll be in trouble with Meemaw."

"We'll be careful," Alex promised.

"Good," Pops said, and closed his eyes and started to snore.

Rose and Alex sighed simultaneously, then went onto the deck and leaned against the railing. It was a very dark night, with only the tiniest sliver of a moon. They couldn't even make out familiar objects, like the blue fountain that watered the white roses, or the ivy-covered archway that led to the alabaster statue of a fawn.

"I still think it was a hummingbird," Rose said.

"An albino hummingbird," Alex remembered. She yawned. "It's possible, I guess."

"Neal said he saw more than one though. There couldn't be more than one albino hummingbird, do you think?"

"I don't know," Alex said. "There's some town in Illinois that only has white squirrels, so maybe we only have white hummingbirds." Her eyelids were drooping and she yawned twice more. "Maybe he's right, and it's some kind of moth."

Rose didn't answer. She leaned over the railing and stared hard into the darkness, willing the little creature to reappear. Tomorrow, she was going to figure out a way to ask Pops about the bird houses - why he put them on the ground. What sort of bird lived in a house on the ground, where cats and snakes and a million other bad things could pop in the front door without an invitation?

"I'm so mad!" Alex complained, covering her mouth with both hands as she yawned again. "I absolutely cannot stay awake another minute. I'm going to take a nap."

"Okay," Rose told her. "I'll wake you up if I see anything."

"Don't fall off, okay?" Alex said, unrolling her sleeping bag next to Pops, shoving her feet in first.

"I won't, I promise," Rose said softly. She wanted Alex to go to bed so she could be by herself. She thought she might be able to figure things out, if she had some time alone in the darkness. Why somebody as mean as Nicole Macavity was so popular. Why Alex had a nice dad who coached her softball team and always gave her a hug if he hadn't seen her for a few hours. Alex's mom was nice too. She was the kind of mom who didn't mind altering blue jeans so they'd fit exactly right. How come Alex had two great parents and she just had a mom who acted like she didn't care if she ever got out of the hospital?

At least I've got nice grandparents who love me, she reminded herself, thinking of Neal's grandparents. And she still had a dad, somewhere, even if he didn't want to be her dad. That was better than knowing he was dead. She knew, too, that one day her mom would get well and come back for her. She wasn't sure where they would go, but she was confident that they would be together. Poor Neal - his dad was gone for good and his mom ... she might be gone for good too. What if he had to stay with his crabby grandparents for the remainder of his childhood?

All of a sudden, the tiny white creature appeared, hovering right in front of her face! It seemed to glow in the darkness, as though the white light came from inside its body. Its wings were so transparent, they were almost invisible, and its tail draped around its legs like ... It wasn't a tail, it was ... Rose squinted at it, afraid to move and scare it away. It wasn't a bird, she decided. It was more like a ...

She blinked and it was gone. She turned to wake Alex, but what would she say - *I saw it again and I still don't know whether it's a bird or a bug?*

She looked down into the garden, watching hopefully as the night air chilled her skin. She just wanted to see it one more time, so she could be the one to announce whether it was an albino hummingbird, a rare butterfly, or a lunar moth.

Suddenly a light flashed towards the back of the garden. Then another, a little closer. Then another and another. Rose held her breath and didn't move, even a fraction of an inch. The lights were flashing throughout the garden, like tiny flashlights turned on and off, off and on. She leaned against the railing and watched with awe - a circle of light formed over the place where she thought the blue fountain must be. It descended, like a giant halo, then rose again.

"Fireflies," she whispered, remembering what Meemaw had said. Sometimes Meemaw said things that sounded so dumb, but later, they happened exactly as she promised they would. She wondered if Meemaw had ever seen the light show, and if that was the reason she had given Alex and Rose permission to sleep on the balcony. If only Alex hadn't fallen asleep so quickly ...

While Rose watched with amazement, the lights flashed in rhythm. It made Rose think of the hymns the choir sang in church – she almost thought she could hear music. A few times, the fireflies streaked across the sky in a band of purple and gold. She wondered if Alex would believe her, when she tried to describe it in the morning.

She tiptoed across the room to find her sleeping bag, then carried it onto the balcony. She crawled into it without making a sound, then stretched out and stared sleepily into the night sky. The flashes seemed to come closer, until she was surrounded by the light, warm and cozy and safe from all harm.

She closed her eyes, wondering when she had ever felt so lucky.

Lucky? She tried to argue with the feeling, but it didn't matter if it made sense. She *was* lucky and she knew it. Luckier than Neal, and maybe even luckier than Alex.

Chapter Eight

"It's gone," Neal said with certainty. "Like it wasn't ever there. Your grandpa must've filled it with putty or something."

"Maybe you aren't looking in the right place," Alex said hopefully, staring up and down the fence line, searching for the hole.

The garden was enormous and so was the corn field - it was impossible to be sure if they were standing in the exact same spot as the day before.

"I've gone all the way up and down this side," Neal insisted. "I've been out here since seven this morning trying to find it."

"I hope my grandfather didn't see you," Alex said. "It would really hurt his feelings."

"I wasn't looking at his dumb garden," Neal said angrily. "I just want to see that moth again."

"It's not a moth, it's a bird," Alex said, glancing at Rose for agreement.

Rose was seated on an enormous rock, staring down a long row of corn stalks at Neal's grandparents' house. She didn't seem to be paying attention to what they were saying.

"It was a moth," Neal said. "I saw it a bunch of times yesterday. You only saw it once, for about two seconds."

"Rose!" Alex demanded. "Are you even listening?"

"Sure," Rose said agreeably.

Alex and Neal frowned at each other over the top of Rose's head.

"How come you aren't talking?" Neal asked.

"I guess I don't have anything to say." Rose pointed her finger between the rows of corn. "I figured out what I'm going to paint."

"What?" Alex and Neal asked together, staring in the direction she was pointing.

"If you sit on this rock, and look through the corn field, you can just see the corner of Neal's house."

"You're going to paint the corner of Neal's house?" Alex said with a confused expression.

"It's not *my* house," Neal grumbled. "It's my *grandparents'* house."

"Who does the flowers?" Rose asked him. "It's got so many colors! Magenta and fuchsia and coral and mauve."

"Fuchsia?" Alex repeated. "What color is fuchsia?"

"Sort of a purply-pink," Rose said.

"My grandma planted the flowers," Neal said with a touch of interest. "My mom said how she can't believe my grandma works in her garden wearing a good dress. She wears gloves, of course, but even so ..." He stooped beside Rose and tried to see what she saw.

"Did she do it before or after your dad ..." Alex slapped her hand over her mouth.

Neal swallowed hard. He tried to remember whether the flowers had been there when his parents went to the marriage seminar.

"Don't you think it would make a good painting?" Rose asked.

"I don't know," Neal said, straightening up and pacing along the edge of the cornfield. "Are you supposed to be an artist or something?"

"I'd *like* to be. I got all this stuff for my birthday - an easel and paints and brushes and paper. But I've been too scared to try it."

"What's so scary about trying to paint a picture?" Alex said. "If it doesn't turn out good, you just throw it away."

"I thought I might have a gift for it," Rose tried to explain. "You know how Meemaw is always saying the secret of happiness is discovering your gift and putting it to good use? I thought painting might be my gift."

"How come you changed your mind?" Neal asked, trying to understand.

"I didn't," Rose told him. "But if I actually try to paint something, then I'll know for sure whether or not I have that gift. And if it's *not* my gift, I'll have to start all over with some other gift, like writing poetry, or building bridges, or baking homemade bread."

Neal grinned, and then he laughed. "Building bridges?" he teased.

Rose shrugged, not at all offended.

"You said you didn't believe what Meemaw said," Alex reminded her. "You said you know plenty of people who don't have a gift."

"I changed my mind," Rose said. "I think a lot of people don't ever figure out what their gift is and maybe that's what makes them so unhappy." She got up and started towards the house. "I'll be back," she promised. "I'm just gonna get my painting stuff."

"That's nice," Alex sighed. "She's going to paint ... what are we supposed to do? Stand around and watch her?"

Neal sat down on the rock and stared down the row of corn stalks. The beautiful flowers planted beside the house were changing his feelings about his grandmother. It didn't seem like either of his grandparents really cared that his dad had been killed. They never talked about him, or about the fateful day when America was so brutally attacked. It was like his dad had never existed. But maybe his grandma *did* think about her only son. Maybe she just didn't talk about him because it made her feel too sad.

"First Rose quits talking, now *you're* doing it," Alex complained.

Neal stared at her, as if he didn't see her. "Sorry," he said finally. "I have a lot on my mind." He stood and brushed his hair back and pushed his glasses higher on his nose. "I wonder if Rose has sketch pads and pencils."

"Meemaw has a ton of craft stuff in one of the closets upstairs," Alex remembered. "I'm sure there are drawing pads and pencils, from when we were younger."

Neal hadn't brought any of his own art supplies along. He hadn't felt much like sketching since his dad died.

Alex led the way back to the house. "I try to let Rose be the one to choose what we do when I'm here," she explained. "My parents say it's nice of me to be so patient with her. They say it's a help to the grandparents."

"Yeah. They probably get tired of trying to cheer her up all the time."

Alex stopped walking. "When I'm at school, I'm a natural leader. My friends are always asking me what to do and they like to check with me before they make any big decisions. But when I'm with Rose, I have to be a different person. Do you know what I mean?"

Neal smiled and raised his shoulders.

"I feel sorry for her," Alex tried to explain. "Especially now, since her mom's in the hospital. But still ..."

"I guess it's sort of hard being her cousin."

"It is," Alex said with obvious relief. "Even if I know it isn't fair that so many bad things happen to her all the time and nothing bad happens to me. You know?"

"No," Neal said soberly. "I'm kind of in the same boat with Rose at the moment."

"Sorry," Alex mumbled.

Neal made a face. "It's not like she's a bad person. And it's not like it's her fault."

"It would be easier to understand if the bad

stuff only happened to bad people," Alex said.

"But it doesn't," Neal said firmly, thinking of his dad. "Bad stuff happens to good people too." He took his glasses off and polished them on the hem of his T-shirt, though he had cleaned them only moments before.

"Do you draw pretty well?" Alex asked him.

"I used to," he said without modesty. "But I haven't tried in a long time."

"It's probably like riding a horse," Alex speculated. "Once you learn how, you never forget."

"Have you ever ridden a horse?"

Alex shook her head. "But who knows - it might turn out to be my gift. Do you think drawing is your gift?"

"My dad used to say I had a natural talent. Do you think that's what Mrs. Cameron means by a 'gift'?"

"It sounds like the same thing."

Neal wondered what Rose would say if he drew something that proved he was genuinely talented. He understood why Alex thought it was hard being her cousin. He rolled his eyes skyward, then crossed them and stuck out his tongue.

Alex covered her mouth with both hands as she giggled.

Then Neal started laughing too, even if he didn't know what he was laughing about. If Rose felt jealous of his talent and it made her give up her dream of being an artist ... there was nothing funny about *that*.

He looked at Alex and saw that her eyes were

watering from laughing so hard. He liked knowing he had caused her to laugh. He remembered how his dad liked to try and make him and his mom laugh. He decided right then that he was going to try to be more like his dad - saying and doing silly things to make people laugh. Maybe it would turn out to be his gift.

Chapter Nine

"What are you going to draw?" Alex asked, leading the way around the corner to the front door of the mansion.

"A lunar moth," Neal said.

They found Rose coming down the stairs, the easel tucked under one arm, an old back pack draped over the other, an empty plastic margarine bowl in her hand. "I've got to get some water," she explained, heading for the kitchen.

"I'll get us some drawing stuff," Alex said, starting up the stairs Rose had just come down.

Neal looked around with interest, now that there was no one to be offended by his curiosity. The furniture looked old, and the colors didn't blend together the way they should. His mother said he had an artist's eye, and it was revolted by a red couch, heavy purple drapes and green scatter pillows. He thought the Camerons must be poor, even poorer than his grandparents suspected. They had probably bought their furniture at one of those thrift shops, that took things people didn't want anymore and sold them to people who couldn't afford to buy things at a real store.

He couldn't help wondering *why* the Camerons were so poor. They were both old, so they probably got a social security check from the government. And Rose said they were caretakers, so they probably got another check for that. According to his grandmother, the Camerons never went anywhere besides church and an occasional trip into town for groceries. It wasn't as if they spent their money on electronic gadgets, or expensive vacations, and it sure didn't look like they spent it on fancy decorations for their house.

"If I make it all the way to the cornfield without spilling the water, it'll be a miracle," Rose stated matter-of-factly, pausing while Neal opened the door for her. "What's Alex asking Meemaw? For something to eat?"

"No," Neal said. "For art supplies, so she and I can draw."

Rose stopped and the water splashed down the front of her shirt. "You're not good at it, are you?" she asked worriedly.

Neal decided it was best to be honest. "My dad used to say I had natural talent."

"That's like a gift," Rose said with depression.

"Not *exactly* like."

"*Exactly* like," she disagreed. "Maybe this isn't such a great idea. Maybe I ought to wait and try out my paints when I'm alone."

Neal shook his head, somewhat impatient with Rose's inferiority complex. "It's not like anybody's first picture ends up hanging at the Metropolitan," he lectured in an adult voice. "I mean, even somebody like Toulouse L'Autrec had to practice before he got good at it."

"Who's Too Loose ... Who did you say?" Rose asked.

"He's a famous artist."

Rose tilted her head and stared up the front of the house, as though searching for the address numerals. "Okay," she gave in. "Just promise you won't look unless I say you can."

"I promise," Neal said without hesitation.

"I'll see you out there then." Rose kept her eyes trained on the water bowl as she tried to hurry away. "Just don't try sneaking a peek over my shoulder," she called, without looking back.

"I wouldn't dream of it," Neal said, rolling his eyes. "Anyway," he said to himself. "A person ought to try lots of things before they decide which one is their gift. Just because I can draw, that doesn't mean I want to do it for my job."

"Maybe you'd rather build bridges," Pops agreed from behind him.

Neal jumped and spun around. "I didn't know you were here," he said guiltily. "Inside. In the room, I mean."

"I shouldn't have snuck up on you," Pops apologized. "I usually make a lot of noise without meaning to. Are you thinking of building bridges?"

"Me? No. But Rose was. I mean, she wasn't actually thinking about it, but she ... Anyway, you're the one who said it."

"Said what?"

"About building bridges. Were you listening?"

"Meemaw says I never listen. She says that's the whole problem, when I didn't even know there *was* a problem."

Neal stared hard at the older man. It almost seemed like Meemaw and Pops acted dumb on purpose. "I meant, were you listening when we were outside and Rose said that if she can't draw, she might have to discover a different gift, like building bridges?"

"I think Rose would be good at helping people understand one another," Pops said thoughtfully. "That's a kind of bridge, don't you think?"

Neal frowned at him. He was pretty sure Rose meant *real* bridges, that crossed rivers and railroad tracks. "Whatever," he said, somewhat sullenly.

"Sometimes it's a terrible burden on young people," Pops said sadly. "You're the only ones who can bring the two sides together. But in order to build a bridge, you've got to do some research. You've got to know what kind of foundation has been laid on both ends."

"I have absolutely no idea what you're talking about," Neal said darkly. "If you mean it's up to me to get my mom to be nicer to my grandparents ..."

"Oh, no!" Pops said, raising both hands. "I didn't mean that at all. But if you *could* help, why not do it?"

"What about me?" Neal pleaded, dismayed when he felt his eyes well up with tears.

"It's *all* about you," Pops said, patting his

shoulder in a comforting way. "The two come together in the middle, don't you see? It makes the middle much stronger."

Neal wondered if Pops had one of those old people diseases that confused him. "Thanks," he said, inching his way towards the door. "I'll wait for Alex outside, I guess."

"Here she comes!" Pops turned to the stairs and within seconds, Alex made her way down with two sketch pads and a pencil case.

"Meemaw says to watch out for chiggers," Alex warned Neal. "Oh hi, Pops. Guess what! Rose is finally going to try her paint set. She was looking across the cornfield at Neal's house and ..."

"It's not *my* house!" Neal said firmly.

Alex glanced at him with raised eyebrows. "At Neal's *grandparents'* house," she corrected herself. "And she saw a picture in her mind's eye."

"That's where it starts," Pops said gleefully. "Next thing you know, she'll be building bridges, won't she."

"Uh, yeah! That's right!" Alex humored him. She gestured and Neal obediently followed her out the door.

67

Chapter Ten

"What's that supposed to be?" Alex wondered, gazing over Neal's shoulder at his drawing.

"I'm trying to draw the white thing, but it's not easy if you aren't certain whether it's a bird or a bug." He held his picture up, tilting his head from side to side. "Maybe it's not either one."

"What else could it be?" Alex wondered. "An albino bat? I know! It's a tiny space ship from another galaxy and they designed it to look like a bird so earthlings wouldn't get suspicious!" She giggled. She looked at Neal's expression, then she turned and looked at Rose. Neither one was smiling. "I don't know why you're both being so serious," she said. She had crumpled five of her own attempts to draw the small white creature.

"Are you going to let us see your painting?" Neal asked Rose. "If you'd rather not, that's okay, but I didn't want you to have your feelings hurt because we didn't ask."

"You can see it," Rose said. "It's not quite done

though." She unclipped the large white paper from the easel and carefully turned it around, holding it by the corners because the paint went to the very edge. "I thought it would be so simple to paint flowers. Just sort of dab the brush in the paint, then dab it on the paper." She sighed.

Neal and Alex stared at it for a long while, then they both seemed to realize they should make some sort of comment.

"You sure captured the colors," Neal said. "They may not look like flowers but ..." He leaned close to the paper and sniffed. "Are you using scented water colors or something?"

Alex came up beside him and bent down to eye Rose's work up close. "You did a good job getting the bird's dimensions right. It even seems like he's flapping his little wings."

"Ha, ha," Rose said without humor. "You're both so funny."

"No, really," Neal insisted, leaning over with his hands on his knees. "It appears to be hovering over the flowers, like it's trying to decide which one will taste the best."

Rose grated her teeth as she returned the paper to the easel. Then she gasped, and placed her hands firmly over her heart. "I didn't paint that!" she nearly shouted. "I did not even *try* to paint the hummingbird!"

"Oh, sure," Alex said, smiling at Neal. "I guess it painted itself."

Rose's face turned red as she stared at the picture. "Believe me or not," she said, slowly and sternly. "I did not paint the ... whatever it is. I didn't even try."

"Why can't you just say 'Thank you' for the compliment and be glad if you found your gift?" Alex demanded.

"The thing is," Neal said, and he sounded angry too. "Even seeing it up close in the picture, I still can't figure out what it is. I don't think it's a bird *or* an insect. Or an alien," he added, glowering at Alex.

"Oh, really?" she snapped. "Then what is it?"

Rose leaned closer to her picture, then stepped back and smiled. "I think maybe there were two albino hummingbirds and they had albino hummingbird babies. Now there's a whole new species and we're the ones who discovered it. They'll probably name it after us."

"*We* discovered it?" Neal challenged her. "You two never would've noticed it if I hadn't pointed it out."

"You didn't *point it out*," Alex disagreed hotly. "It flew right in our faces."

"Because you were bothering me!" Neal reminded her.

"Bothering *you*?" Alex said incredulously. "You were looking into our private garden without permission!"

Rose carefully unclipped the paper again and, holding it away from her body, started towards the house. "I'm gonna show it to Meemaw," she said, more to herself than to her companions. "So she'll know it's not a firefly."

"Maybe it *is* a firefly," Neal said with depression. "Maybe some fireflies grow really huge in this area and your grandmother has seen them before, when she was a kid."

Alex raised her hands in the air and let them drop against her thighs. "I thought you said it looked like a lunar moth."

Neal hunched his shoulders, admitting he didn't know what it was. "Was she always like this?" he wondered, referring to Rose. He thought his own drawing looked too scientific, like an airplane, rather than something alive.

"Like what?"

"I don't know. Different, I guess."

Alex remained quiet for a moment, as if she was thinking about how to answer. "Yes," she said finally, "but since her mother got sick, she's worse."

"What's the matter with her mother?"

"We don't know exactly. She got upset one night and couldn't stop crying. And then she wouldn't talk to anyone, not even Rose. The only thing she said was that she wanted to go to the hospital so they could give her a shot that would make her go to sleep. Then once she got there, she said she'd like to stay and she hasn't ever come back."

"That's awful," Neal said, worried that it could happen to his mother too.

"Were you popular at your school?" Alex blurted out suddenly.

"Not at all," Neal said with a sad smile. "My father was too strict. He wouldn't let me go anywhere unless there were going to be a lot of adults and some of them had to be people he knew.

I think being a policeman made him that way. He said he saw a lot of kids breaking the law - kids my age. He was always worried something would happen to me. He wanted to move someplace like here, where he grew up. But my mom's always been in love with New York City."

"I'm sorry your dad died," Alex said softly.

"Thanks," Neal said. "Are you popular?"

Alex made a sour face. "I wish I could say 'no,' for some reason, but really, I kind of am. I'm just glad Rose and I don't go to the same school, or she'd probably hate me. I keep trying to give her pointers on how to get people to like her, but she won't take my advice."

Neal folded his drawing in half, then in half again. He stuck it in the back of the sketch book and dropped it on the grass. "I wish I'd see it again," he said wistfully. "I wish it would hold still long enough so I could get a really good look at it."

"Me too," Alex said, though she was actually somewhat bored with the bird/bug. "It's not a *bad* thing to be popular, is it?" she asked him.

Neal looked into her eyes, blinked rapidly, and removed his glasses. "It depends on how you act about it," he said, aware that he sounded like an adult who didn't want to answer the question they'd been asked. "I think it's okay if you're not mean to the kids who *aren't* popular. At my school, the popular kids make fun of the kids who aren't popular."

"I never make fun of anybody," Alex said defensively. She kicked a clod of dirt. "But sometimes I laugh when my friends do it."

"I guess it's kind of like your gift," Neal said, in a more scientific voice. "You should try to use it for good."

"How?" Alex asked. She sounded frantic.

"I wouldn't know, since I've never been popular," Neal dodged the question. "I'm starving, aren't you? I guess I ought to go home and eat lunch."

"Meemaw promised to make more cookies. We could fix a sandwich first, if you want."

Neal thought he shouldn't keep eating the Camerons' food, since it was obvious that they were poor. But he didn't want to sit at the table with his silent grandparents either. "Should we carry Rose's stuff inside? In case it starts raining?"

Alex looked up. The sky was blue and cloudless. "I'll get the paints and stuff if you'll carry the easel," she suggested. "Did you really think Rose's painting was good?"

"The moth was terrific." He decided to call it a moth, until they collected enough evidence to prove it was something else. "Maybe she's gonna be better at doing live figures than scenery."

"She'll probably put it all away and never get it out again," Alex said. "That's the way she is. Pops says she can go from 'gung-ho' to 'ho-hum' in less than ten seconds."

"How come she lives with your grandparents?" Neal wondered. "Wouldn't it be better for her to stay with somebody who's more normal? How come she can't go stay with her dad?"

Alex leaned the easel against her shoulder, long

74

enough to scratch her elbow. "She hasn't ever met her dad. He took off before she was born and asked for a divorce through the mail. Then her mom started dating this guy Steven, and he said he was going to adopt Rose, but they broke up a couple weeks before the wedding was supposed to happen."

"How come ..." Neal gave Alex a sheepish smile. He was embarrassed about asking so many questions.

"How come what?" she said. "Rose would probably get mad at me for telling you all this private stuff about her, but it's not like you're going to go to school and gossip. Are you?"

"No," Neal promised. "How come she doesn't live with *your* family? Wouldn't it be better for her to be around other kids and parents the right age?"

Alex tried to imagine living with Rose. "No way," she said, shaking her head hard enough to slap herself in the face with her hair. "That would *not* work."

"I feel sorry for her," Neal said. "I know how awful it is to lose your parents."

"You didn't *lose* your mother," Alex pointed out sternly. "She's just on a trip."

"She's staying indefinitely," Neal said quietly. "I kept asking her how long she was going to stay and she'd just say 'indefinitely.' It's the worst word in the English language. It doesn't mean anything. It could mean forever."

"It's better than if she said she was gonna stay for a year. This way, you can always think she might come back tomorrow."

"Don't move!" Neal said, in a hushed voice. "Don't even breathe!"

"Why?" Alex asked nervously.

"The moth. There's five of them. On the fence. Just sitting there watching us. Anyway, it *seems* like they're watching us."

"I gotta look!" Alex pleaded, turning her head so slowly, she wasn't sure she was turning it at all. "They're not moths," she decided, as soon as they were within her line of vision.

"Then what are they?" Neal demanded with frustration. "They're not birds either."

"They must be ... I don't know. Some kind of ... flying squirrel?"

"I'm going to try to get a closer look," Neal whispered out of the side of his mouth. He moved his foot so carefully, the grass wasn't even disturbed. But before he had advanced even an inch, the first of the tiny white creatures lifted off the fence and ascended upwards, drifting like a dandelion seed. The second followed, and then each of the others. As they rose, they seemed to enter a cloud of white and disappear.

"I'm getting my camera," Neal said, with a determination that almost sounded like anger. "I'm going to sit right here and wait until I get a picture so I can enlarge it and figure out what they are."

"Well, they're not birds," Alex said slowly. "I've never seen a bird do that - just rise in the sky. They weren't even flapping their wings, were they?"

"I'm thinking they might be some kind of insect that everyone thinks is extinct," Neal confided. "If

I had a picture ..."

"I'll go and ask if I can borrow Pops' camera too," Alex decided.

"Does he have more than one? In case Rose wants to help?"

Alex sighed. "I think he has a couple of them. The old-fashioned kind that you throw away after you take all the pictures."

"Meet you back here in five minutes then," Neal said, setting off at a run.

Chapter Eleven

"What are you doing?" Alex asked Rose, when she found her sitting cross-legged in the middle of the living room floor.

Rose had propped her picture against the cushions of the couch, so that it was eye level. "It moved," she said, gesturing with a nod of her head. "I'm watching to see if it moves again."

"What moved?" Alex asked with annoyance. "Can't you ever just act normal?"

"I *am* acting normal. Normal for me." She gestured again. "The thing. The white thing, whatever it is. It's not a bird. Meemaw still thinks it's a firefly, but I don't think it's a bug either."

"What do you mean *it moved*?" Alex demanded, saying each word slowly and clearly. "We already knew it could fly."

"*In the picture*," Rose said, just as slowly and clearly. "It moved from the center of the picture to the left side."

Alex shut her eyes as her head automatically

turned towards the picture. She opened them and studied it for a long moment. "Did you paint a different one?" she asked suspiciously.

"How could I?" Rose asked. "I left my paints outside."

"Maybe it's a light bulb that's going bad," Alex said nervously. "Sometimes they blink for a while before they burn out and that could make it seem like something in a picture was moving."

Rose looked around the room, but the lamps weren't turned on. "Too bad we don't have a ceiling fan, or we could blame it on that," she said. "Where's Neal? Maybe he could think of a scientific explanation."

"There are a lot of them," Alex said, closing her eyes again. Her voice had turned dull, like someone who felt very sick or scared. "We saw five of them sitting on the top of the fence. Neal's gone home to get his camera and I thought we could borrow Pops's camera too. Neal's hoping he can get a good shot of it and blow it up so he can figure out exactly what it is."

"It's not anything we've ever seen before," Rose said with an air of authority.

"Neal thinks it might be something that's supposed to be extinct. Like a prehistoric moth? Or maybe it could be a cross between a bird and a butterfly? Or an ancient species, like a flying chipmunk?"

Rose sighed and got up from the floor, moving as though *she* were ancient. "It's why we aren't allowed to go in the garden," she told her cousin.

"Is that what Meemaw said?"

"No. But I'm sure that's why."

Alex thought about it for a moment. "I think so too," she decided. "Maybe Pops is raising them? Maybe they're part of a top-secret experiment for the government?"

"What would the government use them for?" Rose scoffed.

Alex shrugged her shoulders. "I don't feel all that great. If my parents weren't out of town, I'd ask them to come get me."

"Lucky you," Rose said. "I can't ever call my parents and ask them to come get me."

Alex rolled her eyes. "Do you want to help us or not?" she asked.

"I have one of those throw-away cameras upstairs. I'll go get it," Rose said in answer, trudging across the room to the stairs.

Alex backed into the doorway, as though she didn't want to stand too close to the picture.

"What are you up to?" Pops asked, coming into the room from the other doorway.

Before Alex could answer, or say something to stop him, he sank onto the couch and leaned back on Rose's picture.

"Uh oh! What's this?" he wondered, leaning forward enough to pull it out from behind him. He put it on his knees and tried to smooth the wrinkles away, nodding his head with satisfaction. "I think Rose *has* got a gift for painting. These flowers look so real, I can practically smell them."

"What about the white thing?" Alex dared him.

"What white thing?" he asked, holding the picture at arm's length.

"The not-a-bird, not-a-bug thing," Alex said specifically. "As much time as you spend in the garden, you must have seen them flying around."

Pops pushed his glasses up his nose and moved his head right and left as he scanned Rose's art work. "Don't tell Rose, but I don't see the bird," he whispered. "Where is it? Would you mind pointing it out?"

Alex stomped across the room and pushed the paper flat on his knees again, but the little white creature had disappeared. "That's impossible!" she said angrily. "What kind of paints did you buy her? This is not funny, Pops! Her mom is already crazy!"

"Her mom isn't crazy," Pops said seriously. "Who told you that? Your Aunt Felina made straight A's all the way through school - high school *and* college. She's a lot smarter than I'll ever be."

"I didn't think she went to college," Alex said, continuing to eye the picture with a wary expression. "I thought she quit high school and got married."

"Oh, no," Pops said, shaking his head. "She quit college, not high school. She fell in love, you see. Happens to lots of people. When you fall in love, you forget all about the plans you were making for your future. Your dream sort of disappears, just like that." He snapped his fingers and settled a little deeper into the cushions. "Don't get me wrong," he sighed. "I'd rather fall in love with Meemaw a thousand more times than graduate from college even once. But a person has a job to do, whether or not they're in love."

"Is that what Meemaw means when she talks about figuring out our 'gift'?"

Pops clapped his hands, as if Alex had accomplished something spectacular. "That's right! And it's good to start trying to figure out your gift while you're still young. If Felina could've gone right back to whatever she was meant to be doing in the first place, she would've been fine. But she got mad at herself for getting mixed up. Good thing I don't get mad at myself for that, or Me, Myself and I wouldn't ever be on speaking terms."

He chuckled with amusement, but Alex only sighed and tapped her toe.

"Well, she'll get back to it in time," Pops said, a little more seriously. "And once she gets on the right path - the path that's right for Felina - she'll run into the right person. That's how it works. 'Course, he has to be on the right path too. She might have to wait awhile for him to catch up, but he'll get there sooner or later."

"Do you really think painting is Rose's gift?" Alex asked.

Pops held up the painting so that Alex could see it. "Don't you?" he said with surprise.

Alex turned her eyes to Rose's picture again. "It's really good, isn't it," she said. "You're right - the flowers look so real, they practically smell good." She kneeled down and studied the picture more closely. "I really *do* smell something perfumy. Maybe it's just my imagination?" She looked as if she might cry. "I don't think this is the same picture Rose painted outside. Maybe the white thing got paint on its wings and painted the picture itself. And then it got tired of being stuck to a piece of paper."

"There you go," Pops said with a smile. "Makes perfect sense to me."

"What's my gift?" Alex asked Pops in a small voice.

"Well now, let's see," Pops said, studying her as if he'd never seen her before. "You're pretty. And we already know you're as sharp as a cat's claw. You're a natural born leader, aren't you? People seem to enjoy your company ... maybe you could do something that might persuade them."

"Persuade them to what?" Alex asked. She no longer sounded frightened.

"To what?" Pops volleyed the question back to her. "That would be the part you'll have to figure out."

Alex frowned at him and got up. "Have you got a camera I could borrow?" she asked politely.

"Rose is getting it," he assured her. "One for her, one for you."

"Pops," Alex said, staring into his eyes. "Do you really not know what the white things are that live in the garden?"

"White things? You mean grubs?"

"No! They fly! Meemaw keeps saying they might be fireflies, but they're much too big to be fireflies. You can't ever get a good look at them, because they fly so fast. One time, they got right in our faces, like *they* were trying to figure out what *we* are."

"Imagine that!" Pops said with awe.

"Haven't you ever seen them?" Alex pressed him. "I mean, you're always out in the garden. How come you haven't ever seen them?"

"Maybe I have," Pops admitted. "You say Meemaw thinks they're fireflies?"

"She hasn't actually seen them either," Alex admitted. "We just described them to her."

"Well, maybe she's right," Pops suggested, toeing off his shoes and lifting his legs onto the couch. "I'm going to take a short snooze," he announced. Then he closed his eyes and started snoring.

Alex sighed heavily and turned to go up the stairs, just as Rose appeared on the landing, headed down. "I've got two of those disposable ones," she said, holding them up. "Meemaw said Pops doesn't have a camera. Just an old one but you can't buy film for it anymore. Not around here anyway."

"That's the bad part," Alex grumbled, accepting one of the cameras from Rose. "If we had a digital, we could see it right away. When I go home, I could even put it on the computer and blow it up bigger."

"We'll have to get the film developed," Rose agreed. "Maybe Pops would take us to one of those one-hour photo labs."

"I doubt if it would do any good. Once the film is developed, there won't be any birds or bugs or whatever they are anyway. They'll just disappear - poof! C'mon! Hurry up!" she urged Rose. "Before Neal thinks I started eating cookies and forgot about him."

Chapter Twelve

Neal was seated on a camp stool, and two more were folded at his feet.

"Where did you get these?" Alex asked, setting one up for herself.

"They were here when I got back," Neal told her. "I figured you and Rose brought them out."

Alex looked at Rose, but Rose just opened her stool and sat down. Immediately, she raised the camera to her eyes and began watching the fence, as if looking through binoculars.

"There's a lot of weird stuff going on and it seems like nobody but me is even noticing," Alex said, her voice tight with tension.

"Like what?" Neal asked.

"The bird disappeared out of Rose's picture," she told him.

"No it didn't," Rose corrected her. "It just moved."

"It moved again," Alex said coldly. "Right off the paper."

"Really?" Rose said, but she didn't lower the camera.

"And the flowers really do smell." Alex added.

"What flowers?" Neal asked. He had lowered his expensive digital camera and was peering intently at Alex.

"In the picture. Pops noticed it too. He said they were so realistic, they even smelled like flowers!"

"He did?" Rose said, surprised and pleased.

"Don't you get it?" Alex yelled. "Did you spray perfume on the picture? Why did it smell good?"

Rose shrugged. "Meemaw was holding it. Maybe she had lotion on her hands."

"What happened to the white thing?" Alex reminded her. "Are you gonna come up with some kind of simple explanation for that too?"

"I guess it flew away," Rose said. "Or maybe you just imagined it to begin with. All I know is *I didn't paint it*."

"Could Meemaw see it?" Alex asked anxiously.

"What are you talking about?" Neal asked. His cheeks were pink.

"Calm down," Rose advised, looking first at one, then the other. "Meemaw says God is working in our lives, that's all. She says there's nothing to worry about."

"Oh, that's nice!" Alex bellowed. "Meemaw never worries about anything! She doesn't know you're supposed to worry sometimes!"

"Who says?" Rose asked curiously. "There's no law that says kids have to worry about stuff, except getting their homework done."

"That's easy for you to say!" Alex protested tearfully.

"No it's not," Rose disagreed. "If I wanted to worry, I could find plenty of things to worry about and you know it."

"You *do* worry," Alex accused her. "You just worry about stupid stuff, instead of worrying about the things that are important."

"Like what?" Rose asked, making a face.

"You don't even care if your hair is permed on one side and straight on the other! Do you know how weird you look? I would *never* go to school if my hair looked like that! I wouldn't go anywhere. I would stay locked up in the bathroom until it grew out. I would make my mom bring me my meals on a tray and I'd eat them in the bathtub."

"Calm down or you're gonna end up in the hospital like my mother," Rose lectured.

"Well maybe I don't blame her for wanting to get away from this place," Alex said tearfully, wiping her eyes with her sleeves. "It's downright creepy, that's what it is."

"If somebody doesn't tell me what you're talking about, I'm going home," Neal threatened.

Rose lifted the camera to her eyes again. "The white thing probably came and left ten times while we were arguing," she said. "Pretty soon it's gonna be too dark to take a picture."

"It's probably too dark already," Neal said, noticing that the sky had gone gray.

"Tomorrow is Sunday," Rose announced politely.

"So?" Neal and Alex said together.

89

"We have church in the morning. Meemaw said to tell you you're welcome to go along, if you want to."

"Me?" Alex and Neal said together.

Rose lowered the camera. "Both of you. Either of you. There it is!"

They turned to look and the tiny white creature was hovering between them, turning its head from side to side, as if comparing them in some way.

"It doesn't have wings," Alex said. She was terrified, even if she didn't know why she should be afraid of anything so small and cute. "It has ... arms."

"It does too have wings," Rose disagreed. "It has wings *and* arms."

"Wow!" Neal said. "It looks like a ..."

Suddenly it was gone, as though it simply disappeared into thin air.

"What?" Rose said.

"It looks like a *what*?" Alex prodded him.

Neal opened his mouth, but no words came out. "I don't have a clue," he finally admitted. "What time is church?"

"There you go again," Alex said, jumping up, her arms held close to her body while her fingers clenched into fists. "Like it never happened. Like we didn't just see something really, really weird."

"Nine o'clock," Rose said. "Do you think your grandparents will allow you to go?"

Neal shrugged. "I don't know. Do you leave at nine or does it start at nine?" He glanced at Alex, who was stomping around with her hands on the top of her head.

"We leave at nine," Rose said. "If you want to go and your grandparents say it's okay, meet us at the car at nine."

"Nine it is," Neal said, forcing cheer into his voice.

"Bye Neal," Rose said, equally cheery. "Stop acting so weird," she lectured Alex, leading the way back to the house.

Chapter Thirteen

"How come your grandparents are letting you go?" Alex asked Neal.

Neal had expected them to say no. "Maybe they're glad to get rid of me for a couple of hours," he guessed uneasily. He was wearing navy slacks, a white shirt, and a real tie. Alex and Rose wore blue jeans and short-sleeved cotton sweaters. Rose's hair was curly on both sides.

"Did she get a new perm?" Neal tried to whisper to Alex.

"Meemaw did it with a curling iron," Rose said. "Please don't talk about me like I'm not here."

"Sorry," Neal muttered, making a face. "Isn't your grandpa going along?" he wondered, when Meemaw came out of the house alone.

"They almost never both leave at the same time," Alex explained. "One of them always has to stay home and watch over the house."

Neal glanced at the house as he climbed into the car. The porch roof was sagging, the paint was peeling, and some of the windows were crisscrossed with duct tape. He didn't think it would tempt very many burglars.

"Neal wants to know why you and Pops can't both go to church at the same time," Rose told her grandmother. She watched while Meemaw put the key into the ignition and started the engine, then hesitated, as though she didn't remember how to drive.

"We only have four seat belts," Meemaw explained. "We'd have to strap Pops onto the luggage rack and he'd get an earache from the wind. What did your mom have to say?" She turned her head to smile at Neal. "I take it she arrived safely?"

"Are you talking to me?" Neal asked, glancing at Alex. His mother had called a few moments before he left the house, but there was no way Mrs. Cameron could know about it.

"I didn't talk to my mom," Alex said.

"Neither did I," Rose said, looking out the window with her face pressed against the glass.

"She said she made good time," Neal answered. "She said she's probably going to stay out there for a couple of weeks. But how did you know she called me?"

"You just mentioned it, didn't you? Are you going to attend school while you're here?"

"Oh, yeah. She said that too," Neal remembered. It bothered him, the way Mrs. Cameron answered a question with a question. She seemed like the sort of little old lady who wasn't really very bright, and yet somehow she knew things she couldn't possibly know. It was like a mystery, but for some reason, he wasn't trying very hard to solve it.

"Oh, good!" Meemaw said happily. "Rose will have someone to sit with on that long bus ride."

Neal opened his mouth to protest, but he couldn't think of a good reason to refuse. If he was only going to go to Rose's school for a couple of weeks, it wouldn't matter if he hung around with her. But if he was going to be stuck in David City much longer than that, he'd want to choose his own friends and he doubted he would choose Rose. He wouldn't mind hanging around with her outside of school, since she was sort of interesting. But he felt certain Rose was kind of girl who wouldn't be friends with him at home if he wouldn't be friends with her at school.

The choir was already singing by time Mrs. Cameron and the three children entered the church. Meemaw didn't seem embarrassed, though a lot of people turned their heads to stare at her. She marched past several empty pews and went all the way to the front, where they would have to tip their heads to stare up at the preacher.

A moment later, Pastor Goode climbed up to the pulpit and smiled at the three children. Then he instructed the congregation to turn to Ecclesiastes 7:14 in their Bibles.

Neal didn't have any idea where to find any of the books of the Bible. He and his parents hadn't gone to church very often, and when they did, Neal spent the hour in Sunday school. There had always been a time of worship, even for the children, but it had consisted of a teacher telling them a Bible story, then helping them make a simple craft. He watched Rose and Alex from the corner of his eye and noted that they both found the passage without any trouble. He sighed and opened his Bible to somewhere in Psalms.

"'When times are good, be happy; but when times are bad, consider: God has made the one as well as the other,'" the preacher recited the verse aloud.

So! Neal thought, with an angry toss of his head. God *was* the one behind the bombing of the World Trade Center! He and his mother had argued about it until she was 'blue in the face,' as she put it. *God doesn't do bad things to people*, she had insisted. She couldn't explain why those things happened, or tell him who *was* responsible, but she refused to blame God for his father's death.

He thought back to the memorial service at their church, and all the things people had said to try to make him feel better. *It's God's will ...* That seemed to be the most popular thing to say after a tragedy took place. What kind of God was He, if His will included the death of so many innocent people in a single day? That reminded Neal of another thing people liked to say: *Your father is in Heaven now, with the angels.* "I don't see what's so bad about dying," one of his friends had tried to comfort him. "Just imagine - the streets are paved with real gold!" *So what?* Neal wanted to shout. *What's wrong with asphalt and concrete? Who cares about golden streets when everyone you love is in a different world altogether?*

"Keeping that in mind," the preacher said, "let's

96

turn to Psalm 44, verse 17. 'All this happened to us, though we had not forgotten you or been false to your covenant. Our hearts had not turned back; our feet had not strayed from your path. But you crushed us and made us a haunt for jackals and covered us over with deep darkness.'"

The words struck Neal's heart like a sword. His dad had been "covered over with deep darkness." He had been buried beneath tons of concrete and glass and metal. The urge to cry was so powerful, Neal was afraid he was going to break down. If only they weren't sitting in the very front of the church, where he would be a spectacle for everyone to see! He inhaled slowly, trying to erase all thoughts of his father. He must not listen to anything else the preacher said, unless he wanted to make a complete fool of himself in front of several hundred people.

"Now let's go to the New Testament," the preacher said with enthusiasm. "Beginning with James 1:2. 'Consider it pure joy, my brothers, whenever you face trials of many kinds.' Are we beginning to get the picture?"

Neal was beginning to get a picture he didn't want to see. A picture of his father, buried beneath a fallen sky scraper. He wondered, not for the first time, whether his father had thought about him before he died. *Pure joy?* Neal felt certain he would never suffer more than he had since the first plane crashed into the World Trade Center.

He sat up straight and turned his head to look out the window, but he couldn't see anything because it was stained with color. The jagged pieces of glass formed a picture of a man kneeling beside a huge rock, his face turned up to the sky. It was probably Jesus, Neal realized. He remembered coloring a picture of Jesus one Sunday. He was angry with the people who were selling things outside the temple. He turned their tables over, swinging some kind of whip to chase them away.

Neal was angry too. He wished Jesus would use that whip on the person who ordered those men to fly an airplane into the side of a building, killing a lot of innocent people. It was such a stupid thing to do! To end someone else's life, just because they didn't agree with your opinion about something. The men who flew the airplanes probably didn't even know any of the people they killed that day. Neal decided he would never believe in anything that required him to kill innocent people.

The organ began to play, and he heaved a deep sigh of relief. Four men began to pass the collection plates, and Neal dug in his pocket for the five dollar bill his grandfather had given him. He watched as Rose opened a tattered denim purse and pulled out several wadded up bills. She added them to the offering, then folded her hands neatly in her lap. On the other side of Neal, Alex was busy pushing back the cuticles of her fingernails with the cap from a BIC pen. Beside Alex, Mrs. Cameron was swaying in time to the music.

The urge to cry came again and Neal had to blink hard to keep his tears from falling. He tried to remember why he had wanted to come to church with them...

Because of the white thing. The weird creature that seemed to have human arms.

He wondered what his mother would say if he called her back this afternoon and begged her to come and get him. She would say 'no'. Hadn't he begged her not to leave him behind in the first place? But she had done it anyway.

Everyone stood up and Neal felt a surge of relief that the church service was almost over. When they got home, he was going to tell Alex and Rose he had something else to do today. He would dig a book out of his suitcase and spend the afternoon in his bedroom, reading and eating cookies and drinking soda. That was one good thing about staying with his father's parents - they didn't nag him about eating too many sweets.

Because they don't care if you get sick, he thought, angry with himself for thinking it.

Chapter Fourteen

"So is our church anything like your church?" Rose asked Neal, as they filed down the aisle.

"It's not *my* church," Alex was quick to correct her.

"It's the same religion," Rose pointed out.

"They do a lot of stuff different though."

"Like what?" Meemaw asked with interest.

"They didn't make Neal stand up and turn around so everyone could see him." Alex turned to Neal with a look of apology. "Our church is much bigger," she seemed to brag. "We have three services every Sunday morning."

Neal barely listened as Alex went on. He didn't care about her church or how popular she was at her school. He no longer cared about figuring out what the white thing was either. It was probably a lunar moth, just as he'd thought from the beginning.

After hanging around with the crazy neighbors for two days, he was acting crazy himself. He didn't really believe that Rose's picture had changed by itself, and he didn't believe that the flowers she painted had a fragrance. It was probably some kind of practical joke. All of it. Including the white thing. It was probably done with a projector. Mr. Cameron was probably operating it from the third floor balcony.

The minute Meemaw put the car in park, he thanked her for taking him and jumped out. "I can't do anything the rest of the day," he told the girls, speaking firmly so they wouldn't argue.

"I'm going home this afternoon," Alex warned him with an unhappy frown. "I thought we were going to ... you know." She whispered the last, nodding her head at her grandmother.

"I can't," Neal insisted. "Nice meeting you, Alex. Maybe I'll see you again sometime."

He had planned to go straight into the house, but he was afraid his grandparents would stop him on the way to his room. He didn't want them to see him crying. He didn't want to answer questions, or say something polite about the church service. He walked slowly, until he was sure he was out of sight, then ran for the clubhouse as fast as he could go.

"I will not cry, I will not cry," he recited, pacing back and forth, his hands clenched into tight fists. He should've known going to church was a terrible idea. It reminded him of those first days, when everyone said they were praying. He had prayed too. He had made a million promises to God, if only his dad would be all right.

Finally he gave in and covered his face with his

hands. "Why?" he asked. "Why? Why? Why?" The pain came over him in a great wave, and he sobbed with misery. "If he had to die, why did he have to die like that?" he asked the God he didn't believe in. He thought he had asked that question a thousand times, even if he had never spoken the words out loud before.

"Meemaw made me come," Rose said from the doorway.

She had startled him, and he looked at her before he thought to turn away and hide his tear-stained face.

"She knew you were crying. I guess she figured out that the minister said a bunch of stuff that would make you feel bad."

"I wasn't crying," Neal said. He took off his glasses and wiped his eyes with his fists. "I didn't listen to what he said anyway."

"He's really nice," Rose went on, keeping her eyes averted. "He wouldn't have hurt your feelings on purpose."

"He didn't hurt my feelings," Neal said angrily.

"He said some good stuff too." Rose stepped inside the clubhouse and looked around. "About having hope for the future."

"That's nice for you," Neal said in a sour tone. "Your mom will get better and your dad will come back and you'll all live happily ever after."

"It's possible," Rose said, lifting her chin, as though she had been imagining just that. "Don't you believe in miracles?"

"No," Neal said without hesitation. "I don't believe in anything."

"You have to believe in *something*," Rose argued. "Everyone believes in something."

"Well I don't."

"Don't you believe in God?"

"No. Why should I?" Neal backed up and sat down. He forced himself to breathe slowly through his mouth, determined not to cry anymore.

"That's the way I was when my mom first got sick," Rose said. "I decided not to believe in Him anymore. I mean, it seemed like the more I believed, the worse things got."

Neal was curious, in spite of himself. "How come you started believing in Him again?" he asked. "It's not like anything got better, unless you're glad you have to live with your grandparents."

"I *am* glad of that," Rose said emphatically. "What if I didn't have any relatives and I had to go in an orphanage? Or if Alex was my only cousin and I had to go and live with her?"

"I thought you *liked* Alex," Neal said with surprise. He had been jealous of the friendship the two cousins shared, and wished he had a cousin of his own.

"I *do* like her, but I wouldn't want to live with her. Would you? I mean, she's the most popular girl at her whole school! Everyone would be watching me all the time, to see if I was like her."

Neal suspected people would be watching Rose all the time anyway. "How come you started believing in Him again?" he repeated his question.

Rose shrugged. "I missed Him."

"You *missed* Him?" Neal said bitterly. He

rolled his eyes and shook his head.

"When you're all alone in the world, like I am ...
Well, sort of alone. I have the grandparents but
even when they're there, they're not there, if you
know what I mean."

Neal nodded. He thought it was a perfect
description of Rose's grandparents.

"He's my best friend," Rose went on, suddenly
shy.

"God?"

"Jesus. Jesus is God, but I like to think of Him
as Jesus, because He lived here, on Earth, so He
really does know exactly how I feel."

"Some best friend," Neal said with biting
sarcasm. "He takes your dad away and then he
takes your mom away and then your grandma
gives you a permanent that only curls half your
hair."

"Actually, she got a phone call right in the
middle of doing it and when she came back, she
squirted the first side twice and didn't do the other
side at all." Rose came the rest of the way into the
clubhouse and sat down on a rock. "This is really
cool," she said with approval. "Did you build it
yourself?"

"It's nothing special," Neal said, unwilling to
talk about his dad.

"I'm surprised your grandparents let you," Rose
said honestly. "Did they take you to the hardware
store to get the stuff?"

"My dad built it," Neal said gruffly. "When he
was a kid. Then, last time I was here, a couple
years ago, your grandpa gave me the stuff to fix

it." Neal remembered how frightened he had felt when Mr. Cameron approached him. Now he thought Mr. Cameron was the least scary person he'd ever met.

Rose nodded. "That's how he is. Always helping people."

Neal remembered the day his parents returned from their marriage counseling weekend. He and his dad had sat across from one another, just as he and Rose were sitting now. His dad had cracked a few jokes about the comfortable furniture. If Neal could remember them, he would tell them to Rose, to try to make her laugh.

"How can you not believe in God?" Rose asked softly. "Isn't it sort of scary?"

Neal frowned at her. "I have a scientific mind and the whole concept of God doesn't make sense to me. If there *was* a God, things would be different, wouldn't they? Horrible things are happening to people all over the world every single day. Even to children."

"Those things would still happen if there wasn't a God," Rose said logically. "Suppose God decided to move to some other Universe and leave us on our own. Do you think people would stop getting sick and cars wouldn't crash into each other and nobody would get divorced? All the bad stuff would still happen. Dads would run away from home and dads would die and moms would still have nervous breakdowns. Everything would be the same except we wouldn't have God to comfort us and make us strong enough to live through it."

"God doesn't make me strong," Neal argued defiantly. "He makes people *weak*."

"Nope," Rose said with authority. "You're weak because you don't have Him. And I'm strong, because I do."

"If you're an example of strong, then I'd rather be weak," Neal snapped. He wanted to say that she hadn't suffered as much as he had, but he wasn't sure it was true.

"Okay, have it your way," Rose said, unaffected by his cruel words. She stood up and backed into the doorway, smiling at him.

Neal wished he hadn't been mean to her. All of a sudden, he didn't feel like being alone.

"Hey, Jesus," Rose said, as though there was someone else in the clubhouse with them. "This is my friend Neal. He's having a terrible day. Please try and help him, even if he does say he doesn't believe in You." She stepped outside, then leaned her head back in. "Just talk to Him," she advised Neal. "It's worth a try, isn't it?" She turned and headed for the corn field, singing the hymn from church, just loud enough for Neal to hear.

"Hey, Jesus," he repeated with scorn. "Rose is a dork!"

Suddenly he felt warm. *Too* warm. He unfastened his tie and fanned his face with both hands. He wondered if he was running a temperature. "Oh, great," he complained. "Now I guess I'm gonna get sick."

He noticed how quiet it was. Perfect silence. Nothing was moving, like the moment just before a storm.

"Hey, Jesus," he said again. He guessed it couldn't hurt to try it. "I really miss my dad!" He sniffed a few times. "And my mom," he added. "I'm worried she's going to have a breakdown, like Rose's mom, and she won't be able to come back to get me." He sniffed again. Then he bowed his head and folded his hands and listened.

Chapter Fifteen

"There's your father's clubhouse, the summer he finished it," Neal's grandfather said, resting his finger on the edge of the picture. "He used to love to spend the whole day out there reading those Hardy Boy mysteries."

"I didn't know he liked those," Neal said with interest.

"They were actually left over from my childhood," his grandpa chuckled.

"Here he is with your mother," his grandma said. She was paging through a different album, one that included his father's college days. "He brought her home to meet us. He was so proud! He knew we would like her."

"And we did," his grandfather said with satisfaction. "Here's his go-cart. He built it from scratch and entered it in a contest. Took a third place ribbon. There were what, about two hundred entries?" he asked his wife.

"Oh, more than that! There were people who

came all the way from St. Louis and Kansas City, as I recall."

"They built the track on a hillside, so those carts had to carry the boys up a steep slope." His grandfather smiled and nodded his head, almost as if he could still see it. "Most of them quit."

"But not your dad's," his grandmother said proudly. "His went right up without a cough. Afterwards, he gave it away, to a children's home in Arkansas. Here's a picture. Every one of those boys put his hand on the cart, as if they were all saying it belonged to them."

"I wish he would've saved it for me," Neal said wistfully.

"He wasn't much older than you when he built it," his grandfather laughed. "He wasn't thinking he might have a son someday." He closed the album and took his handkerchief from his pocket. He blew his nose, then pushed his chair away from the table. "I'm going to go turn on the news, see what's going on in the world," he told his wife.

"And I need to make a grocery list," she said, closing the cover on her album too. "This was so nice," she told Neal. "Thank you for asking to see the pictures. I was afraid to look at them by myself."

"Maybe we can look at them some more tomorrow," Neal suggested. "I'm going to go and see what Rose and Alex are doing, okay?"

"Sure, honey. I'm glad there's a boy next door for you to play with."

Neal started to correct her, then decided it didn't matter. It was funny, he thought, how nothing had changed, but everything was different.

He went out the back door and headed towards the corn field. He wondered if he could build a go-cart from scratch. Of course, there wasn't really anyplace in New York where a boy could ride a go-cart. Maybe he could build something else. Maybe he could create a new computer game, or build a robot and enter it in the science fair. And then he could give it away to an orphanage, or one of the public schools in an area where the kids looked really unhappy.

He knocked on the front door and Alex opened it almost immediately.

"Pops said you were coming," she said, gesturing for him to come in. "I asked him how he knew, since he wasn't by the window, and he said he recognized the sound of your footsteps."

Neal just smiled. "Where's Rose?" he asked, following Alex into the living room. Mr. and Mrs. Cameron were seated on the ugly couch, rolling skeins of yarn into balls.

"Good thing you're here to take my place," Pops said, holding out his hands. The yarn was wrapped from one hand to the other in a figure eight, and he carefully transferred it to Neal's hands. "Meemaw is going to sew an afghan," he said proudly.

"You don't *sew* an afghan, you *knit* it," Alex corrected him with good nature.

"Or crochet it," Neal told her.

"Now, how would you know about a thing like that?" Meemaw asked, as if he'd just quoted a complicated mathematical formula.

"My mom crochets sometimes," he explained. He tried to remember the last time he had seen his mom crochet or do counted cross stitch or work on her quilt. Mostly she just sat on the couch and stared out the window.

"Sometimes it helps to get away for a while," Meemaw said softly. "When you come back, it's easier to make a new start."

Neal just smiled. "Where's Rose?" he asked again.

"She's gone to see her mother," Meemaw told him. "Felina called this morning, while we were at church. She asked for Rose to come and visit this afternoon."

"Felina is Rose's mom," Alex explained.

Neal knew he looked surprised. He had given up on Rose's mom. He had believed she was going to stay in the hospital forever. Now it looked like she might get well after all, and come back to claim her daughter. No wonder Rose believed in miracles.

"When Rose went to visit last time, her mom acted like she didn't even know who she was," Alex told him. "So Rose didn't know if she woke up this morning and suddenly remembered she had a daughter and asked to see her, or if it was the doctor's idea."

"It wasn't that Felina didn't know who Rose was last time," Meemaw told Neal. "She was taking a lot of medications that made her feel sleepy and confused."

"But now she's better," Alex said.

"Would you call that a miracle?" Neal asked

Mrs. Cameron.

She smiled at him. "You're very good at this," she said, nodding her head at his hands. "Is it a natural talent, or have you had practice, doing it for your mom?"

"She doesn't roll her yarn into balls," he said patiently. "Can almost anything can be a miracle?" he pressed.

"Everything *is* a miracle," Meemaw said with a smile.

"Not everything," Neal disagreed, remembering the rubble where the World Trade Center used to stand.

"If the very worst thing that ever happened to anybody turns into something good for everybody, then is the good part the miracle all by itself?" Meemaw asked him.

Neal mulled it over, while Mrs. Cameron kept working and Alex sat watching him from the floor. He thought they were both very wise, since they knew when to keep quiet.

"Anyway," Neal said. "When is Rose coming back?"

"We don't know," Alex replied. "If the visit goes well, she might stay all afternoon."

"When are you leaving?" Neal asked her.

"Soon. My parents are stopping by for me on their way home and their plane was supposed to land at two."

Now that he didn't want to be alone, it looked as if he would have the whole afternoon to try to entertain himself.

"Look," Mrs. Cameron said, sweeping her hand

towards a trash bag beside her chair. It was obviously filled with skeins of yarn. "Or Pops might need some help in the garden."

"Fat chance!" Alex snarled. "Sorry, Meemaw, but if his own grandkids aren't allowed in the garden, I don't think Pops is going to let Neal go in!"

"Maybe not," Meemaw said thoughtfully.

Alex seemed satisfied and got up from the floor with a happy expression. "I think I heard a car door," she said. "I'm going to go up and get my stuff."

The moment she disappeared, Pops hurried into the room. "Neal!" he hissed, just as the last few inches of yarn slipped through Neal's fingers. "I need your help outside! A cat has gotten into the garden!"

Neal jumped up and ran, following Pops through the kitchen, through the mud room, down a long flight of stairs to a sort of porch with dingy windows. Then Pops opened the back door and ushered him outside, into a world of brilliant colors.

There were flowers everywhere, of every imaginable size and shape and hue. Yellows and reds and blues and oranges and purples ... and every shade of green that could possibly be imagined. The smell was wonderful, and so strong, Neal wondered why he hadn't been able to smell it next door.

"Follow me," Pops said urgently, starting off down a narrow path, bordered by landscaping timbers and filled with small white rocks.

Neal had to struggle to keep up, and he marveled at the older man's agility. There wasn't much opportunity to look around as he passed through the various areas, and he vowed to walk more slowly on the way back, even if Pops went on ahead without him.

"Here kitty!" Pops called, as they came into a small clearing. "Here kitty, kitty, kitty!"

"Here kitty!" Neal called too. This was the area he had seen through the hole in the fence. There were large bird houses all over the ground, with tiny fences marking off something like yards around them. Neal turned in a slow circle, trying to estimate how many houses there were. Dozens. Dozens and dozens.

"Here kitty, kitty!" Pops called. But he was really just standing there, watching Neal.

"There it is," Neal said. It was a big yellow cat with green eyes and it seemed to be smiling at him. He knew how tricky cats could be - they'd allow you to come within inches before they darted out of reach. "Hi kitty," he crooned softly, holding out his hand, so it could smell his fingers. "What are you doing in Pops's garden?"

"Oh, it's not *my* garden," Pops said merrily. "It's *God's* garden. Don't you know, all gardens belong to the Lord? He's the only one who knows how to put the color and smell into the flowers."

Neal knelt down beside the cat and lifted it up in his arms. "And the white things?" he asked, without turning to look at Mr. Cameron.

"They live here, in the little houses," Pops explained. "It's a whole city, you see. They serve the entire state of Missouri and parts of Oklahoma and Arkansas as well."

"What do you mean, they 'serve'?" Neal asked softly. The big yellow cat was heavy in his arms. It lolled against his chest and rubbed its chin against his collar, as if he was adorned with catnip.

"Just like we do," Pops explained without explaining. "I take care of the garden - that's the way I serve. And you served by helping Rose."

"*I* helped *Rose*?" Neal said with surprise, turning around to look at him.

Mr. Cameron's eyes were twinkling as he bobbed his head up and down. "She tried to help *you* and that helped *her*."

"So *I* helped her by letting her *try* to help me," Neal clarified. He thought about it, while he scratched the cat under its chin. He wanted to serve, but he didn't want to serve by letting someone else help him. Still, if it really had helped Rose ...

"And you helped your grandma and granddad," Pops went on, with a tone of respect. "Asking to see pictures of your dad when he was your age. Now *they* can start to heal."

Neal hadn't mentioned that, but he didn't waste time wondering how Pops knew about it. "What about my mom?" he asked.

"She'll be fine. It's like Meemaw said - sometimes it's just good to go away for a while, so things seem different when you come back. Your mom is very strong. You don't have to worry that she'll fall apart on you."

"Why did ..."

"Felina fall apart?" Pops sighed and ran his fingers over the top of his head in a habit left over from the days when he had hair. "It was my fault," he said guiltily. "I showed her the garden before she was ready. I thought it would help."

Neal looked around him, somewhat fearfully. If something in the garden had made Rose's mother go crazy, he wasn't sure he wanted to see it.

"Don't worry - you're ready," Pops said, and waved his arm, as if introducing someone.

Suddenly the tiny doors of the bird houses began to open and the little white figures began to come out. They mostly stood about in clusters, chatting and gesturing towards Neal.

"What about the cat?" Neal worried.

"Hold onto him," Pops advised.

Some of the white things began to fly, and a few of them hovered near Neal's face, giving him a closer look.

"They're little people!" he said with excitement.

"They're angels," Pops said. "Assigned to duty on Earth. The garden is where they come between assignments, to rest up. Of course, there are millions of gardens like this one all around the world. Well, not millions. But thousands, I guess. Or maybe just hundreds."

"I don't know why, but ... I didn't think angels would be so small," Neal whispered. He was crying, even if he wasn't sad. Tears were streaming across his cheeks, but he couldn't stop smiling.

"They can be any size they want to be," Pops explained. "Or I guess it more depends on what

117

size they *need* to be. They can be a hundred feet tall or they can look just like you and me."

Neal hesitated, wary of asking the question that was waiting on his tongue. "Are you an angel?" he said, so quietly, he almost didn't hear himself. "You and Meemaw?"

Pops laughed. "Goodness, no," he said. "We're just caretakers! I'm the property caretaker and Meemaw ... it's her job to take care of me. And she does, doesn't she. Those cookies ... yum! They're the best chocolate chip cookies in the entire universe, wouldn't you agree?"

"Yes," said Neal without hesitation. He knelt down, still clutching the cat in his arms.

"You can let him go," Pops said. "He won't hurt them."

"Do they talk?" Neal wondered, releasing the cat, who immediately began to wash its face.

"To each other. When they're our size and they're wearing blue jeans and driving cars, then they talk to us."

"If they're angels, does that mean ... Do you think maybe they might have ... seen my dad?"

Pops frowned, as if he was trying to figure out a sum. "I'm not sure," he finally said. "But I do know that your dad is okay, Neal."

"How do you know?"

"I just know. I can't tell you how I know, because I don't really understand how it works. But that's okay. It's enough just to know."

Neal understood that he could either believe Pops or not. He *wanted* to believe him, but he wasn't sure it was all right to believe in something just because you wanted it to be true.

"He wasn't running away from you," Pops said quietly. "That image you keep seeing? Where your dad is running toward the buildings? He was running to try and help the people who were trapped inside. That was his job, you see. His way of serving. He chose it, and when the time came, he did what he was meant to do. But I *can* tell you this, Neal - his feet were heavy. They were as heavy as that rock furniture in your clubhouse. He had to work harder than he ever worked before to run down that sidewalk into the smoke. Because he knew he was leaving you and your mom and his parents behind."

"How could you know about ..." Neal hadn't ever told anybody about the movie that played in his head. He had seen a policeman on the news, in one of the film clips, and thought it was his dad. He had wanted to reach into the TV and stop the man and turn him around and make him run the other way because he knew the buildings were going to collapse any minute.

Suddenly the angels joined hands and lowered their heads. Neal glanced over his shoulder and saw that Pops had bowed his head too, clasping his hands together as if he were going to pray. Then suddenly, the silence began, just as it had in the clubhouse that morning. It was so powerful, Neal could scarcely breathe. Something had come. Something or Someone Wonderful. And Good.

He closed his eyes and tried it on, like a new shirt. What would it feel like to know, really *know*, that his dad was in Heaven and that he was all

119

right? What if all those things people said to him at the memorial service were true?

And then he *did* know. They *were* true. His dad was okay. He was okay and Neal would see him again someday. *He knew it was true.*

"Isn't it amazing?" Pops whispered.

"It *is* amazing," Neal said. "Is this a miracle?"

"It *is* a miracle," Pops agreed. "Yes, indeed, that's just what it is – a full-fledged miracle."

Chapter Sixteen

"Here's the part I don't like," Rose said. She was seated on one of the camp stools, trying to paint a picture of the fence. "We're going to forget. Probably within the next few days."

Neal laughed. He was trying to draw a picture of his dad from memory. "Are you kidding? I'll *never* forget what I saw!"

"Yes, you will," Rose said. "That's the way it works. Pops said."

"I don't *want* to forget!" Neal protested. "Why should it work like that? Why would we have to forget?"

"Because we'd tell people and no one would believe us. They'd think we're crazy. They might even lock us up, like my mom."

"Did she tell you that's why she got sick?"

"Not exactly," Rose sighed. "Here's what I think - she didn't believe in God anymore, because too many sad things happened. She didn't *want* to believe, just like you. And me too, for a while anyway. She decided to forget God and just live the wild life. I'm not sure what she was planning to do, but I have a feeling it wasn't something good."

"Is that why Pops showed her the garden?"

"Maybe. I don't know exactly what he was thinking. I just know he's only supposed to do it if the angels tell him he can. But he was so worried about my mom, he decided to do it anyway. He figured the angels would understand once he explained it, but he couldn't explain it *before* he took her in the garden because he knew if he didn't take her right then, she was going to pack up and leave for good."

"But you didn't know *what* happened," Neal said, imagining how scary it must have been.

"I just knew what I heard," Rose remembered with a shiver. "I woke up in the middle of the night and I heard my mom yelling at Pops. She kept saying, 'They aren't real!' but I didn't know what she was talking about. And then she yelled, 'I hate You!' and that probably scared me worse than anything."

"I don't know how anybody could hate your grandpa," Neal said honestly. "He's the nicest person I've ever met."

Rose beamed at him. "She didn't mean Pops. She meant God. She was *that* mad at God."

Neal winced. "That's scary," he said.

"Not really," Rose said with nonchalance. "God understands how we feel. He expects us to get mad at Him sometimes. Anyway, Pops thought maybe the angels could reason with her. But she wasn't ready to see them, so it made her go crazy."

"She remembers though," Neal pointed out. "She didn't forget what she saw."

"She will," Rose sighed. "When she comes home tomorrow, she'll tell Pops he ought to put the bird houses up on posts or trees, in case a cat ever gets in the garden. That's how he'll know she forgot." Suddenly she tore the sheet of paper off the pad and crumpled it. "I'm not meant to be an artist," she said glumly. "Now I have to start all over trying to figure out what's my gift."

"You don't have to figure it out right away," Neal said. "You've got years before you have to choose a major for college."

"It feels really important though," she tried to explain. "Like if I find the answer to that, I'll be able to figure out the other stuff too." She sat quietly for a few moments. "Maybe you're right," she said slowly. "Maybe I could just have fun for a while, before I decide."

"You could come to New York for a visit," Neal suggested, though he wasn't sure his mom would go along with the idea. "You and your mom."

"Me and my mom?" Rose said with surprise. "You think our moms would get along?"

Neal hadn't ever met Rose's mom and she hadn't met his mom, but somehow he knew they would all get along. "For our sake," he said. "Because they love us and want us to be happy."

Rose rested her hands on her knees and stared up at a cloud that had muted the bright sunlight. "Do you think we'll remember *some* of it?" she

123

asked hopefully. "Like the part about seeing some sort of little bird or bug that we couldn't identify?"

"We have to remember *something*, or else how did we get to be friends?"

Suddenly Rose smiled. "You know how I told you about Nicole Macavity at my school? The day I went to school half-permed, she was making fun of me on the bus and guess what ... a big white bug flew in the window and landed in her hair!"

"They were watching over you all the time," Neal said. He knew it meant they would watch over him all the time too.

"Lucky Alex," Rose said. "She never knew about the angels so she won't be sorry to forget them."

"Let's not be sorry about it anyway," Neal suggested. "Let's just be glad we got to know for a little while. And when we forget, we won't be sad, because we won't know what we forgot."

Rose laughed happily. "Thanks! Duh ... why didn't I think of that?"

Neal closed the cover on his sketch book. "I was reading the Bible last night," he said. "It's really hard to pronounce the people's names."

"I don't even try," Rose admitted. "I think people back then even got tired of trying because most of the names in the New Testament are easier."

"I was looking for verses about angels," Neal went on, rather seriously. "I wanted to pick one that would always be a special reminder of that day in the garden." He and Pops had remained in the garden for a long time. Neal had been allowed to peek inside the tiny houses and see that they had small appliances and couches and bedrooms. He had wanted so much to talk to one of them, but Pops said angels only spoke to humans when directed by God, and that Neal no longer needed their help. "You want to hear the verse I memorized?" he asked Rose.

"I'll bet I can guess it," Rose said. "I think I might be a little like Meemaw because sometimes I can guess what people are going to say." She was quiet for a moment, while she squinted up at the sky. "He will give his angels charge over you, to keep you in their care? I'm not sure that's exactly right."

"I like that one too," Neal said cautiously, "but that's not the one. See, Peter was in prison, and an angel came and got him out. That's how it seemed to me since my dad died. Like I was in prison."

"And the little angels got you out," Rose guessed.

"No, *you* did," Neal said. "*You* got me out."

"*I* got you out?"

Rose pretended to be shocked, but Neal knew she was pleased.

"So do you want to hear the verse?" he asked impatiently.

"Yes," she said. She closed her paint box and turned around on her stool and looked at him.

"The angel told him to 'Put on your clothes and sandals. Wrap your cloak around you and follow me.'"

"I like it," Rose said, "even if I don't understand exactly what it means."

"Good," Neal said with relief. He wasn't sure he understood it either, but he knew he would do it when the time came, just as his dad had done.

Rose stood up and gathered her paint things in one arm, releasing the easel's catch so that she could carry it under the other arm. "Guess what Meemaw was doing when I came outside?"

"Baking some of the world's best chocolate chip cookies?" Neal said hopefully.

"Yep. And she's going to fix a jar for you to take home to your grandparents."

"And I'll bet they'll be nice about sharing with their grandson," Neal grinned. He closed the camp stools and balanced them on top of his sketch pad. "Whatever happened to the painting you made that had the angel that moved around on the paper?"

"What angel?" Rose asked. She turned to see his face, then she laughed with great gulps of silliness. "I was just kidding," she admitted. "I didn't forget yet, did you?"

"Forget what?" Neal asked, crossing his eyes and sticking out his tongue.

The End

Made in the USA
Middletown, DE
19 December 2024